She met his gaze and she was captivated.

Imaging what it would feel like to be in his arms for just one night. It was dangerous ground to be treading on because she knew that she was falling for him, but she could just have one night of pleasure with him.

Maybe then she could get him out of her mind and focus on work.

Maybe then she wouldn't imagine herself staying with him and then it wouldn't hurt so much to leave.

Even though she knew she shouldn't, she just wanted one night with Atticus. Just one night to chase away all the bad memories of betrayal from Walter. She wanted to cleanse her soul. Atticus's kiss from a couple nights ago still burned against her lips.

At the time she had pushed him away because she thought it was for the best, but now she wasn't so sure.

She wanted this moment.

She wanted tonight.

Dear Reader,

Thank you for picking up a copy of Penny and Atticus's story *Winning the Neonatal Doc's Heart*. It's my thirty-fifth book and I can't believe I've hit this milestone.

I had to set this milestone book in a couple places I actually love so much, the Northwest Territories and Alberta. Fort Little Buffalo is a fictional town nestled somewhere between Fort Smith and Hay River.

Penny is an absolute sweetheart, strong and sassy. She's just been burned one too many times by love.

Atticus is also very untrusting of people and has gone into hiding back where he grew up. He has no interest in a happily-ever-after, until his energetic sled dog takes a certain liking to a new doctor in town.

I hope you enjoy Penny and Atticus's story.

I love hearing from readers, so please drop by my website, www.amyruttan.com.

With warmest wishes,

Amy Ruttan

WINNING THE NEONATAL DOC'S HEART

AMY RUTTAN

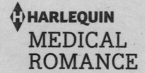

HARLEQUIN
MEDICAL
ROMANCE

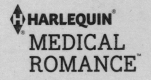

HARLEQUIN®
MEDICAL
ROMANCE™

Recycling programs
for this product may
not exist in your area.

ISBN-13: 978-1-335-73779-3

Winning the Neonatal Doc's Heart

Copyright © 2023 by Amy Ruttan

All rights reserved. No part of this book may be used or reproduced in any manner whatsoever without written permission except in the case of brief quotations embodied in critical articles and reviews.

This is a work of fiction. Names, characters, places and incidents are either the product of the author's imagination or are used fictitiously. Any resemblance to actual persons, living or dead, businesses, companies, events or locales is entirely coincidental.

For questions and comments about the quality of this book, please contact us at CustomerService@Harlequin.com.

Harlequin Enterprises ULC
22 Adelaide St. West, 41st Floor
Toronto, Ontario M5H 4E3, Canada
www.Harlequin.com

Printed in U.S.A.

Born and raised just outside Toronto, Ontario, **Amy Ruttan** fled the big city to settle down with the country boy of her dreams. After the birth of her second child, Amy was lucky enough to realize her lifelong dream of becoming a romance author. When she's not furiously typing away at her computer, she's mom to three wonderful children, who use her as a personal taxi and chef.

Books by Amy Ruttan

Harlequin Medical Romance

Portland Midwives

The Doctor She Should Resist

Caribbean Island Hospital

Reunited with Her Surgeon Boss
A Ring for His Pregnant Midwife

Baby Bombshell for the Doctor Prince
Reunited with Her Hot-Shot Surgeon
A Reunion, a Wedding, a Family
Twin Surprise for the Baby Doctor
Falling for the Billionaire Doc
Falling for His Runaway Nurse
Paramedic's One-Night Baby Bombshell

Visit the Author Profile page
at Harlequin.com for more titles.

For my dear fighter Sharon. Keep up the good fight.
You are an inspiration.

CHAPTER ONE

Hey, can we talk?

I really don't have anything to say to you.

Look, be mad at me, but I need your help on a case.

DR. PENNY BURMAN SIGHED at the sound of texts buzzing on her phone. She should really tell her lying, cheating ex Walter no, but if she helped with a case, then she could show the board of directors in Calgary that she was serious about her job. That she didn't want to leave it and she wanted to come back.

That she was more than her personal embarrassing mistake.

Penny wasn't going to punish patients because Walter had broken her heart, lied to her about being married and the thrown her under the bus. Only she, Walter and the board of directors knew what had happened.

Her mother didn't even know and didn't need to know that she'd made such a foolish mistake.

One she'd never make again.

So she'd told her mom it was her choice to come

up to the Northwest Territories. The last thing she wanted to do was disappoint her mother and tell her she came up to the north because she'd had her heart broken, not knowing the man she was falling for was already married.

Fine, she texted.

Thanks, Pen, he texted back. I'll send you the case later. I miss you.

She didn't know why Walter wanted her on the case. He was the big shot specialist.

She was just a new attending. She'd passed her boards only a year ago.

Ignore the imposter syndrome.

Penny sighed again and pocketed her phone, realizing she'd lost track of time and where she was on her morning jog.

I really hope a bear doesn't leap out at me.

Penny laughed at the absurdity of that thought. Sure, she was in the Northwest Territories and further north than she had ever been in her life, but just because her geographic location had changed didn't mean that her chances of meeting a bear here were any different than meeting one in Calgary.

Calgary had bears.

Just like Fort Little Buffalo, where she was currently working for the next six months, had bears.

Maybe not quite the same.

Penny stopped jogging to check her heart rate monitor and catch her breath. It was colder here than in Calgary for September. That was something she wasn't looking forward to. She was used to cold winters, having spent her life in Alberta, but she wasn't relishing the idea of her first winter here in the Northwest Territories.

Of course, she wouldn't have been in this predicament if she hadn't foolishly ignored her lifelong conviction that love was not real. That true love didn't really exist. She'd let down her careful guard over her heart, and look where she ended up?

Brokenhearted, humiliated and feeling like a complete fool.

Her hospital had turned on her and suggested, for PR reasons, that she take a leave of absence and work in the north at a smaller hospital Calgary often partnered with while they kept on the brilliant pediatric cardiothoracic surgeon from Toronto they had been wooing.

The man who had shattered her heart.

A married man.

Penny cursed at herself under her breath and continued on her run. She'd be done with this run if she could just ignore Walter's texts.

It's for a patient. He's texting you about a patient. Remember that.

For a patient, she could talk to Walter.

She was still so angry with herself for falling for Walter. She knew better. She had taught herself better than that. Her mother had been the other woman, and her father had chosen his wife and other children, who were in the process of emigrating to Canada from India to join him, over her and Penny. Once her father's wife and other children came to Canada, Penny's father left.

Penny missed her father.

Sometimes.

He'd been in and out of her life in her early years, but she hadn't seen him since she was in high school.

When he didn't bother to show up to her graduation.

She'd been so certain he would. She'd worked so hard academically for him.

She'd seen the pain and heartache her mother had been through. Her mother was the daughter of Indian parents, but had been born and raised in Canada. So even though her parents both had the same heritage, they'd grown up in completely different worlds. Her mother grew up here and her father in India.

Her father had a whole other secret life her mother never knew.

Penny never wanted to feel the kind of pain that had plagued her mother's life.

Avoiding that pain guided her to protect her heart.

She was never going to be duped.

And yet she had been.

Now she was here for six months while Calgary appeased Dr. Walter Scott's wife, who wanted Penny far from her husband. Dr. Scott's wife, who was rightfully angry, had a large trust fund, and she planned to donate a lot of money to the children's hospital in Calgary, but only if Penny disappeared while things cooled down.

Penny had had no choice.

You could've quit.

She shook that thought from her mind. There was no way she was going to quit. She wasn't giving up her job as a pediatric physician and surgeon. She'd worked too hard for everything she had. She'd worked three jobs to get through university. Worked for every grade to get scholarships, to better her life.

To prove to her largely absent father that she was worth something.

Only, it was never good enough.

She was never good enough.

Her mother would question her quitting.

Her mother never questioned her decision to come here.

There was a rustle to her left, a crunching in the fallen yellow birch leaves, and Penny froze.

Great. A bear. Just perfect.

Penny reached down for the can of bear spray she carried in her pocket, on the advice of her landlady. She was at the ready for a hungry bear that was prepping for its long winter nap.

She saw a flash of fur bound from the brush.

Okay. This is the end.

Penny screamed and dropped the can of bear

spray as the furry beast leaped up and started licking her face.

"Horatio! Down!" came a loud command.

The licking stopped, and Penny was able to collect herself enough to realize that her assailant was sitting on its haunches in front of her, its big pink tongue hanging out the side of its mouth. One blue eye and one brown eye stared up at her.

It was a husky type of dog. That was her assumption just glancing at the jolly-looking fellow, but Penny was by no means a dog expert. She'd never had a pet growing up, though she'd always secretly wanted one.

Then life, school and everything else got in the way. It had been a long time since she'd thought about having a dog or devoting time to an animal. And that was the crux of it. School and then work ate away at all her time.

Her heart stopped racing as she stared down at it. It held out its paw, looking for a handshake, as if it was introducing itself.

"Horatio? I assume that means you're male?" Penny asked the dog.

Horatio cocked his head to one side, licking his big black nose. Penny knelt down and petted his head. He closed his mismatched eyes and took a swipe at her chin with his big pink tongue.

"Horatio!" came the gruff command again.

Penny stood and saw a mountain man coming out of the forest, looking frustrated. It was like he'd stepped out of the pages of a book. He had on a red flannel shirt, the sleeves rolled up so she could see every inch of his muscular and tanned forearms. His jeans were tight, and he had scuffed work boots on.

He had a well-kept sandy-brown beard and longer hair that was held back with a worn baseball cap. His face was deeply tanned, with a smattering of faint freckles from working out in the sun.

Penny's heart skipped a beat when she noticed his dark brown eyes and their gazes locked. She held her breath as he seemed to pierce through to her very core, making her tremble. Something deep inside her was telling her that this man would be trouble.

Warmth crept up her neck, and she pulled her gaze away from his intense one. She was not going to let herself be swept away by another handsome face. That's the last thing she wanted. Her time here was a punishment of sorts, but also a way for her to work and not have everyone pointing and staring at her for getting involved with a married man.

Fort Little Buffalo was her chance to prove herself again and concentrate on work. It was not a holiday, and it certainly wasn't a time to get involved with a local. No matter how good-looking, rugged and sexy he was.

You don't know him. Think with your head. He's probably involved with someone else.

She wasn't going to get sucked into another scenario where the relationship would prove to be futile. Penny had no plans to stay in the north. Calgary, and the hospital there, were her home. It was there she could truly prove herself and move on to bigger and better things. Even if it meant working with Walter again. She'd learned her lesson. She wouldn't be swayed again by him.

Calgary had more opportunities than Fort Little Buffalo.

This place was just a means to an end.

"Is this your dog?" she asked.

The man only responded with a curt nod and gave the dog a sharp command, which she didn't recognize. Horatio looked disappointed and slinked over to sit beside him.

"He didn't hurt you?" the man asked, reaching down to pet his dog, and Horatio appeared relieved that he wasn't in too much trouble.

"No. Just surprised me, that's all."

The man didn't say anything. Just nodded again, and an awkward silence fell between them. She didn't know what to say, but suddenly she had a feeling that she was the one in trouble. Of course, she often felt that way. She was sometimes too good at sucking in everyone's emotions around her, and there was troubling brewing inside this stranger.

Nothing dangerous, but something sad.

Something that ate away at him.

"I don't usually meet up with other people on this trail this early," he stated. "Horatio and I usually have it to ourselves."

The tone was accusatory, making her hackles rise.

"Last I checked, this was a public trail. Of course, I am new here."

"I gathered," he said.

It was apparent that the dog was more friendly than his human counterpart. The stranger just stood there, and she wasn't sure how to extract herself from this awkward conversation.

She was never very good in these kinds of uncomfortable situations. Kids she understood, but sometimes she really didn't get adults.

"Well, I guess I'll be on my way."

"You going to be here often?" he asked.

"Why?"

"Just so I can avoid another encounter," he replied gruffly. "I'm trying to train my rescue dog, and he's too distracted by…"

"By friendly people?" Penny asked, with a hint of sarcasm.

Really, who did this guy think he was? King of the park? He didn't respond, just gave another command to his dog and stormed off.

Penny watched them leave and shook her head.

"It's so nice to meet you!" she called out. She watched as he froze in place, but he didn't look back.

Great. Just what she needed. Her first encounter

with one of the locals in the place she was going to call home for the next six months, and it wasn't the most pleasant. Especially when the winter would soon be coming and she would be stuck in this town. Nothing could be more isolating than not being on good terms with the few people who lived up here.

Penny hoped that the rest of the residents of Fort Little Buffalo weren't like Horatio's ornery and grumpy owner, or it would make for a long six months.

Penny got back from her run and tried not to think about the handsome grump she had met out in the park. Right now, she had to make a good first impression on her boss. That was something she prided herself on, good first impressions. Even though this wasn't where she wanted to be, she was going to do her best.

Like she always did.

And she was curious about who her boss was.

She had only managed to see on her papers when she was in human resources that the chief of pediatrics was a Dr. Spike. There were no initials, but she wondered if it was the world-famous Dr. Atticus Spike. He was the guy who had revolutionized pediatric surgeries across the Eastern Seaboard and who had mysteriously vanished five years ago from Boston after a surgery had gone wrong.

Not that the mistake had been his.

Far from it, but losing one of the conjoined twins when you were recognized as a world leader in separating twins must've been a hard blow to handle. It had been a highly publicized event because the twins mother was an influencer and their father was a rock legend. The whole world had been following their progress.

The surviving twin was left paralyzed.

The world mourned with the parents, but Dr. Atticus Spike just vanished.

Penny had always thought that was shame. The papers he wrote had been brilliant. He was a bit of an idol of hers.

There was no way on this green earth that a famous surgeon like Dr. Atticus Spike would ever pick Fort Little Buffalo in the Northwest Territories to work.

In the end, it didn't matter who the chief of pediatrics was. She just wanted to make a good first impression and get to work.

Her scrubs were freshly pressed, and she smoothed back her hair one more time in the rearview mirror of her car. She took a deep calming breath, but her heart was racing.

No one knows about your indiscretion, Penny, and no one cares.

And that's what she had to keep reminding herself of. She was worthy of being here. They wanted her here.

"Father, I got first place in the science fair!"

Penny had exclaimed over the phone. *"You can come visit and see my ribbon!"*

"Your brother got a place in the National Science Fair. Did you?"

"No... But..."

"Well. Try harder."

She got out of her car and locked the door. She was a pediatric surgeon. She hadn't been one for very long, but she was talented, and she could handle this minor bump in the road. There was a game plan in place now to ensure she'd never make that mistake again.

Penny held her head up high as she made her way into the hospital and straight for the pediatrics department, where the chief of staff was waiting for her.

"Dr. Burman, it's a pleasure to see you again," Dr. Lance Wood said brightly.

"The pleasure is all mine, Lance. Thank you for having me here."

"Nonsense. We're thrilled that a surgeon of your caliber agreed to come up here and fill in for Dr. Thorne while she's on maternity leave. Atticus will be glad for the competent help."

"Atticus?" Penny asked, trying to swallow the excitement that was bubbling up inside her.

"Yes. Are you familiar with his work?" Lance asked.

"Yes, if you mean the Dr. Atticus Spike who revolutionized vascular surgery in neonates?"

"Indeed," came a gruff voice from behind her. "You can cut the fawning, though. That life is behind me."

A chill ran down her spine as she recognized that voice. She turned around slowly and came face-to-face with Horatio's sexy, albeit grumpy, owner.

Her idol.

Her new boss.

Dr. Atticus Spike, and he looked none too pleased to make her acquaintance again.

Atticus was never happy when a new doctor from the south joined the staff. There was always the threat that they would know exactly who he was, and then they would flatter him, hoping that they if they buttered him up enough, he would take them under his wing, and once they got what they wanted from him, they would cast him aside.

Just like his ex-fiancée, Sasha, had.

Don't think about her.

He'd been so in love with Sasha, and he thought she had loved him too, but when the hospital in Boston had turned their backs on him during the investigation into the twin's death, so did Sasha.

It had nearly destroyed him.

There was no one he could trust.

So, he was already grumpy about that and the fact the new doctor seemed to recognize him. What he wasn't expecting was the new doctor from Calgary to be the gorgeous woman he had run into this morning.

Or rather the woman Horatio had run into.

Horatio was a reckless rescue and was still learning how to behave in polite society.

So when Horatio bounded off, Atticus hadn't been expecting to run smack-dab into a woman who took his breath away.

It was like someone had come up and kicked him square in the chest. She was the most beautiful woman he had ever seen. She wore her black hair pinned up, and he couldn't help but wonder how long it was and how it would feel running through his fingers.

Her large dark almond-shaped eyes, with long, thick lashes, drew him in. She was tall and graceful, and her designer jogging gear screamed *city*.

It took all his control to hold back, because he knew she was new in town, or possibly passing through, and he had promised himself after having his heart broken by Sasha that he was never going to get involved with anyone again.

And once he had made his mind up, that was it.

His father always said he had a stubborn streak, and it was that stubborn streak that had served him well when he was practicing medicine on the smallest patients. It also protected his heart after it had been crushed by betrayal and deceit.

So he was none too pleased to see that the new doctor he would be working with was the mysterious woman from the park whom Horatio took a liking to. Even worse, she knew exactly who he was, which meant she would totally kiss his ass.

And he didn't need that kind of adoration. Sasha, a pediatric neurosurgeon who'd worked with him, had been like that when they'd first met, and it was all an illusion.

He didn't want to deal with it again, which was why he'd returned to his hometown instead of moving to another big hospital. Atticus just wanted to be left alone.

"You? You're Dr. Atticus Spike?" There was a hint of disbelief and maybe derision in her voice.

He was surprised and fought back the urge to smile. Maybe she wouldn't be that sickeningly sweet adoring fan after all, because by the look of shock on her face and the blush that rose in her high cheeks, she was not too pleased to see him.

Not that he could really blame her.

He had been quite grumpy with her in the park.

"One and the same," he said gruffly.

"Atticus," Lance said, a warning tone in his voice. One that Atticus knew well, because he had managed to drive off every young pediatric surgeon in the last couple of years.

Although it wasn't completely Atticus's fault.

Some of those other doctors had left of their own accord when they'd realized that Atticus and his reputation weren't going to get them anywhere.

Atticus could spot a user or manipulator from ten miles away. That he was certain of.

"So, you're the surgeon from the south?" Atticus asked.

"Calgary," she said, her eyes narrowing, and she crossed her arms. "I was part of a prestigious program, and I'm very well-versed."

"Dr. Burman was the youngest to graduate in her class from the University of Alberta in pediatrics," Lance said, smiling. "We're so fortunate to have her."

That was a warning to Atticus. He snorted, acting like he wasn't impressed, even though he really was, but he wondered why she was here and not in Calgary.

That's not your business.

And it really wasn't. He didn't want to get involved with her life. As long as she was a competent physician and they could work together, then he didn't care what she did in her personal life.

Don't you?

There was a little part of him that wanted to know if she had a partner. If there was someone waiting at home for her. Someone who took her in their arms and kissed those luscious lips. Heat surged through him as he thought about it.

He knew one thing. He had to put distance between himself and Dr. Penny Burman.

"Well, you can help with the first shift in the emergency room. There are a lot of colds this time of year, fall allergies and the like," Atticus said, shoving his hands in the pockets of his white lab coat so he wouldn't be tempted to reach out and tuck back that little wisp of hair that had escaped her bun.

You need to get a grip.

He had to keep as far from her as possible.

"That sounds spectacular," Penny said stiffly. She turned to Lance, who handed over her identification and a pager. She was amused they still used pagers up here, but her cell service was spotty so she understood why. "If you'll kindly point me in the right direction, I'll start my shift."

Atticus tried not to smile. She was definitely no wallflower and wasn't acting like she was all hurt because he didn't want to be her best friend forever. Maybe he was wrong about her, though probably not.

He never was. Lonely, but never wrong.

"I'll take you there," Lance said. He gave a warning glance to Atticus as he led Penny to the emergency room.

Then Atticus smiled to himself as he admired her. Her back was ramrod straight, and she held her head up high. She turned back once, and their gazes locked again.

His pulse quickened as her dark eyes narrowed on him, full of dislike.

It made him sad, but it was for the best.

It really was.

CHAPTER TWO

WHAT WAS THAT old saying? Something about never peering behind the curtain? Penny wished she had heeded that warning and never met Dr. Atticus Spike, because her first impression of a physician she had admired through his work was completely shattered.

Why were all surgeons like that? Walter had been so full of himself too.

Although she'd been duped by his charm and debonair smile and hadn't seen it at all.

She hoped she wasn't like that when she made a name for herself, but she was sure of one thing. Dr. Spike was an arrogant jerk face.

She chuckled to herself. Her father, who was an English literature professor in Vancouver, would be horrified by her insult.

"Really, Penny. You're an educated woman... have some class," she could hear him say.

He wanted her to be a perfect lady, but that was definitely hypocritical on his part, because he was anything but a gentleman when it came to his dealings with her mother.

Penny shook thoughts of her father out of her head.

He was the last person she wanted to think about.

Especially on her first day at work in Fort Little Buffalo. She may have made personal mistakes in Calgary, but she wasn't going to make them here. She had to work with Dr. Spike, but that was it.

Their relationship would be strictly professional, as all her other relationships in the hospital would be. Penny had learned her lesson. The only people she could trust were herself and her mother.

Her phone pinged, and she read the text from Walter.

Hey! Have you checked over the info I sent you?

Penny groaned.

No. Working.

I'm trying to work too. Please check your email.

Her heart hurt. It was so cold and detached. She had thought he loved her.

I just started my shift. I'll get to it. I promise.

Thank you. You're wonderful.

Only she didn't feel wonderful right now. How could she ever really make a clean break if he was constantly messaging her?

She picked up the next chart that the nurses had

left at the nursing station. Fort Little Buffalo was not a busy hospital, not like Calgary, but there were a lot of outlying villages, and people traveled a distance to get help, so she would be kept busy.

Which was good for keeping her focus on work, but bad because she didn't like seeing kids sick. It felt so good to help them and get them healthy again.

"Hi. Marcus?" Penny asked, reading the file as she opened the curtain surrounding the bed.

The little boy looked so small on the big bed. He was sweating profusely and for a five-year-old boy was acting pretty listless. His cough wasn't a whooping cough, so she ruled that out.

He didn't have a fever and had been tested to see if the infection was viral with a rapid antigen test, but it wasn't, so Penny could see the boy and not have to hide behind a surgical mask.

Marcus gave her a weak smile, but then curled up against his mom, who was in the bed with him.

"I'm Dr. Burman," Penny said, taking the chair next to the bed. "What brings you in today?"

"Asthma. At least, I think it's asthma. Our village hasn't had a doctor in four years, but the last time a doctor visited, he mentioned that it could be asthma. I was told there would be a follow-up, but never heard anything."

Penny made her notes. "And what made this doctor think it could be asthma?"

"I thought Marcus had pneumonia again. When

he was born, he had it," Marcus's mother said. "I have a puffer for him, but he's been relying heavily on it lately."

Penny took the inhaler from the mother and made note of the medicine. "He's been having the max amount of dosage, and he's still struggling?"

Marcus's mother stroked her little boy's head. "He gets so jittery."

"Yes. It's common with the albuterol, but it won't harm him." Penny handed back the inhaler. "I'm going to order some tests with our respiratory team. You're going to stay put, because I know you've traveled far. So I'm going to admit you. We'll get these tests done as soon as possible, and I'm going to arrange for an allergy test."

"Does it hurt?" Marcus asked, wheezing.

Penny got up. "No. Allergy tests have changed a lot. It won't hurt. You might have some itchy spots on your arm, but we can give you something for that. Now, can I listen to your chest, Marcus? Is that okay?"

Marcus nodded and sat up.

Penny slipped the stethoscope on and listened to his chest. She could hear his wheezing. She couldn't say it was asthma, not without all the tests, but there was something there. There was something impeding his ability to breathe.

Penny took off her stethoscope. "I think I'm going to order a chest X-ray. Just to make sure that his chest is clear."

Marcus's mother said, "Thank you, Doctor."

"Depending on how long the tests take, I think I would like to admit him for now. Just so we can keep a close eye on him and you can stay with him."

Marcus's mother visibly relaxed, looking relieved. "Thank you. We came from five hours away by plane…"

"I understand." Penny smiled. "I'll get everything ready. We'll find out what's going on."

Penny slipped out and closed the curtain behind her. She wrote up her orders and gave them to the nurse in charge, who would take care of making sure that Marcus was admitted for observation while the tests were administered.

If they were in Calgary, they wouldn't have admitted him, but here there weren't a lot of options, and according to Marcus's charts, on his arrival early this morning he'd had a low oxygen level.

They needed to watch him.

"An allergy test?" a voice asked with interest behind her. She knew that it was Mr. Jerk Face himself.

Her jaw tightened, and she gripped the pen tighter. "Yes."

"Who is going to administer that? We don't have an allergist on staff."

"I can administer it. As part of rounds at the Calgary children's hospital, I worked with on-staff allergists. If you have the equipment…"

"We don't," Dr. Spike said quickly, but there was a hint of sadness in his voice.

"You don't have the means to do that?" she asked, surprised.

"Yellowknife or Hay River would have it," he stated. "We could have it brought in by plane, if it's urgent."

Penny worried her bottom lip, and then handed him the chart. "The patient and his mother flew in early this morning from a remote village. The boy has been breathing badly for years and a locum doctor passing through suggested he might have asthma, but nothing was ever done. The doctor didn't follow-up."

Atticus frowned as he looked through the chart. "It is urgent."

"I would say so."

Atticus smiled, and it was the first time since she'd met him that he actually cracked a smile. Maybe Mr. Jerk Face did have a heart after all.

"Okay, well then, I will call Hay River and Yellowknife, but they may not be able to send one down. How do you feel about flying?"

"I'm used to flying. Why?" Penny asked.

"I can take you."

"What do you mean, you can take me?" she asked dubiously.

"I am a certified bush pilot, and I have a plane. You have admitted the patient, correct?"

"I have…" Penny was still in shock. Atticus Spike was a pilot?

"Well, when our duty shift is over and the next shift comes on, I'll fly you up to Hay River or Yellowknife, and we'll get what you need to administer the test tomorrow."

"Okay."

"So make the calls and then come find me." Atticus walked away with his charts, and Penny just stood there, stunned. Just a few hours ago, he'd been a closed off backwoods guy with an awesome dog. Then he'd been a grumpy, sullen doctor, and now he was being this super helpful supportive colleague?

It made her dizzy.

He was definitely a guy who blew hot and cold, and Penny really didn't know what to make of it. She rubbed her temple. Her phone buzzed again, but she ignored it.

She didn't have the time for Walter, and it annoyed her. She wanted to help because it was a patient and it would look good in the eyes of the hospital board, but she didn't want to talk to Walter.

"Are you okay, Dr. Burman?" Nurse Rachel asked as she took her seat on the other side of the nursing station.

"I. Think. So," Penny said carefully. She shook head and straightened. "Can you get me in touch with the immunology departments at Hay River and Yellowknife? Tell them it's urgent."

Nurse Rachel smiled. "Sure thing. I'll patch the call through to you when I get a hold of them."

"Thank you." Penny took the rest of her charts and made her way to her next patient. She was so used to having everything at her disposal.

In Calgary, if you needed something from another hospital, it was couriered. Here you had to fly to get the most basic things.

Flying didn't bother her, but being stuck in a plane with Atticus when she really didn't know him and couldn't figure him out was a little much. Hopefully he wouldn't annoy her further and cause her to reach across the cockpit and strangle him.

She laughed at that thought.

At least he has faith in you. He didn't try to dissuade you.

Penny appreciated that. Atticus didn't know her from the next physician, and yet he was willing to take a risk that she knew what she was doing. There had been some times in Calgary when her chief of surgery or the board of directors wouldn't take a chance on her ability.

Probably because Atticus doesn't really have a choice.

She hated that uncertainty was lingering under the surface of her strong facade, and she was annoyed at herself letting that thought creep into her head. She'd worked hard to fight it all her life. Every time she couldn't impress her father, and then falling for Walter, like a fool. Penny shook that thought from her head. She had a job to do, and she was going to do the best damn job she could.

Even if it meant climbing into a bush plane with a man who annoyed her.

When Atticus had offered to fly Penny, he couldn't quite believe the words that were coming out of his mouth. The only people he ever flew in his plane were his sister, her husband or his nieces, and his dog, Horatio.

That was it.

Yet here he was offering to take the very woman that he'd sworn he was going to avoid up to Hay River or to Yellowknife.

It's for a patient. Think of that.

And if he thought of it as part of the job, then he could rationalize it all in his head. She was just his colleague. Granted, a gorgeous one at that.

All through their shift in the emergency room, he would watch her. He just couldn't tear his gaze off away from her, and he was annoyed by that.

Hadn't he learned his lesson with Sasha? When he'd first met Sasha, he couldn't stop looking at her either. The only difference was that Penny didn't seem to pay him much attention or smile at him like Sasha had when they'd first met.

Penny didn't look up at him or flirt, which was a relief in one way.

She seemed focused on her work and her phone.

In fact, her phone seemed to be distracting her, but she looked annoyed by it.

It's not your business.

Except it was.

He was head of pediatrics.

Atticus made his way over to her reading through her notes at the nurse's station. She was alone and didn't seem to notice him.

"Is everything okay?" he asked.

"Fine," she responded, not looking up. "Nurse Rachel said Hay River has what we need."

"Fantastic." He took a deep breath. To admit that he thought she was looking at her phone too much was to admit that he couldn't take his eyes off her.

Why was he so drawn to her?

Why couldn't he talk to her like the other medical staff members in his charge?

"Is that all?" Penny asked, looking up. He was so close to her that he could see the flecks of gold in her dark brown eyes and how her thick black lashes curled to perfection.

He took a step back. "You seem…distracted."

Penny sighed. "The phone? Sorry, it's another surgeon from Calgary."

"Oh?" Atticus asked.

"Just asking for some help on a few cases, but I'm focused here, Dr. Spike."

It was one at first, but now seemed to be a few more.

"Okay." Although something told him she wasn't

happy to help out this other surgeon at all, and he had a sense that she needed to prove herself here.

Atticus had glanced at her résumé. Penny was more than qualified. She didn't need to prove herself here.

"We'll go to Hay River tonight." He wanted to tell her that he could help her adjust, that he knew what it was like to come to a new place and not know anyone, but he didn't say it.

When he went to Boston, he'd been a little lost, but he'd gone there to be the best, to climb to the top. So much so, he'd lost sight of who he was and who he could trust.

Penny nodded and picked up her folders. "Sounds good."

She left, and Atticus took a deep breath. Annoyed he was letting her into his head.

For the rest of their shift, he avoided her at all costs. When the next rotation came on, he found her, gave her directions to his plane hangar, and told her that he would meet her there in an hour.

Atticus closed his eyes and cursed under his breath as he readied his plane. At least they were only flying to Hay River and they didn't have to fly to Yellowknife. Hay River was only a forty-minute flight.

Which meant less time spent in close quarters with Penny.

"What kind of plane is that?"

Atticus turned to see Penny there. She had a couple of coffees in her hands. She had changed into jeans and a gorgeous lilac sweater that hung off her shoulder, exposing a delicate collarbone. Just the sight of that exposed shoulder made his blood heat.

Focus on the task at hand.

"Do you know much about planes?"

"A bit," she said. "I grew up in Calgary, but my grandparents had some land in the foothills. They would often have bush pilots stop in. So I'm used to being around them."

"Have you ever flown in one?"

"Not for a long time." There was a nervous edge to her voice.

"I'm a good pilot," he said.

"I don't know that." There was a twinkle in her eyes, and he couldn't help but smile.

"True. You don't know me other than for my notoriety," Atticus responded gruffly.

"That seems to bother you. Why?"

"I'm more than just my name, and…" he trailed off, because he didn't want to think about Sasha and all the so-called friends he had trusted in Boston. He didn't want to give those people the time of day.

"And what?" Penny asked.

"It doesn't matter," Atticus said quickly, and he finished his prep. There was a part of him that was mad at himself for being so grumpy with her, especially when he'd offered to help her, but it was better this way. She was only here for a short time, and he didn't want to make friends. Still, he also didn't like being this perpetual grump, which he was known for.

As much as he hated it, it was better to drive everyone away.

Penny handed him a coffee cup. "I didn't know what you liked, so it's black."

"Thanks," Atticus said, melting. He was appreciative that she'd brought him coffee. "I like it plain like this."

"I prefer tea." She took a sip from her cup. "Can I help with anything?"

"Not much needs to be done except wait for our takeoff time. I filed the flight plan, and I can borrow my buddy's truck in Hay River to get us to the hospital."

"So, you going to tell me what kind of plane this is?" she asked.

"Why do you want to know?"

"I'm trying to make small talk. I'm not one for awkward silences, and I'm sorry, but this hot and cold thing you've been playing with me since we met, I hate it."

He chuckled softly. "Do you?"

"Indeed." She took another sip of her tea. "Look, I admire your work, but if you think that I'm after something from you, I'm not. I'm here to work, and that's it."

"Why?" Atticus asked.

"Why what?"

"Why are you here to work?"

"That's not your business. All you need to know is that I take my job seriously and I'm a damn fine surgeon."

He smiled again. He had no doubt of that. She had spirit, and he liked that, but there was a part of him that wanted to know why she was here, because there had to be a reason. She didn't seem like the kind of person who would leave a big-city hospital and come to work up here. It was apparent Penny was devoted to her career. So much so, she was still connected to Calgary.

Just like Sasha had been so obsessed with her job. But unlike Sasha, Penny didn't seem interested in using him to further her career.

Which he found refreshing.

So, Dr. Penny Burman was a complete mystery. He always did like a good mystery in his past, but now he didn't like that he was so intrigued by her.

"I don't doubt it." Atticus finished the coffee. "Well, we should probably load up and head out."

Penny threw her cup in the garbage. Atticus opened the door to the plane and took her hand, helping her up inside. Her skin was soft, and tingle of heat rushed through him. He let his hand linger as she took a seat. Even though he shouldn't.

It was nice to touch someone, but he needed to let go. This was dangerous.

He pulled his hand back, trying not to look her in the eye.

A slight pink tinged her cheeks. "Thank you."

He didn't say anything, just nodded and shut the door.

He walked around the plane and climbed into the pilot's seat, slipping on his headphones. "You have a set there."

Penny grabbed the pair of headphones and put them on.

Atticus started his plane and slowly taxied away from the hangar. He spoke with the tower and waited for his clearance to take off. Penny didn't seem nervous at all; in fact, she seemed kind of relaxed.

At least that would make things easier.

"Rebel One, you're cleared for takeoff," the tower came over his radio.

"Roger that," Atticus said. He increased his speed and began his process for taking off. It was a beautiful afternoon, but by the time they headed for home, it would be dark. According to all the weather reports, they would have good weather tonight, too.

In reality, this whole process shouldn't take long, and he hoped he hadn't cursed himself by thinking that.

Penny laughed softly.

"What?" he asked.

"Rebel One? Sounds very sci-fi to me," she teased.

A smile tugged at his mouth, and he couldn't

help but contain his glee that she understood the movie reference.

"Impressive," he said, impersonating a certain scuba breathing villain from the franchise.

Penny laughed, and he liked the sound of her laughter.

It was refreshing.

Penny was slightly nervous about being locked in a plane with Atticus for forty minutes, because she didn't know him, didn't know if he was a good pilot. Furthermore, she meant what she'd said to him. She wasn't sure if she could take his hot and cold attitude.

She had to remind herself that this was for a patient.

Right now, Penny just had to figure out what was causing the boy's allergies.

There was an awkward tension in the cabin of the airplane. Only the sound of the engine and props filled the void.

"It's a Murphy Rebel," Atticus suddenly said, jarring her from her thoughts.

"What?" she asked.

"You asked me before what kind of plane this was, and I'm telling you it's a Murphy Rebel."

"Oh."

He glanced over at her. "Oh? That's all you have to say?"

"What would you like me to say?" she asked.

"Well, I thought you would have more to say than just 'Oh' after asking me multiple times what kind of plane this was."

"I'm not familiar with this kind of plane."

"Then which ones are you familiar with?"

"De Havillands and Cessnas. Those are the planes that I went in when I was younger."

"And what do you think of this?" he asked.

"It's a fine plane. I'll form a better opinion of it after we land."

Atticus chuckled, and it made her heart skip a beat to hear him laugh. Maybe he did have a sense of humor after all. Her father certainly didn't, and Walter had never been the most jovial.

"You should laugh more often or at least try to smile. It makes you seem more human rather than some kind of robot," she teased.

"So I've heard," he grumbled.

They both shared a smile then. Her pulse began to race, She really liked it when Atticus was smiling and laughing. When he seemed to be more real and not so much of a jerk face. She turned and looked back out the window, admiring the scenery.

"We're flying over Wood Buffalo. If we had more time, I would fly over Alexandria Falls, but we're on a bit of a mission."

"That's okay." She wanted to say *maybe another time*, but she held that back. There wouldn't be another time. She was not here to form connections or relationships. Taking someone on a flight to see a waterfall was something friends would do.

Or lovers.

Heat rushed into her cheeks, and she shook that thought away.

She wasn't going to let that thought into her head. Atticus was her superior and experienced, famous, just like Walter, and look where that had got her.

She had to keep Atticus at arm's length. She knew nothing about him, and that was for the best. So instead of focusing on how beautiful and romantic the forests of the sub-Arctic were, she focused on the trees and the water they were flying over. Suddenly, he made a turn, and they were over a large plain in the middle of the forest, with swathes of white over the green-and-brown ground.

"What is this?" she asked in shock. "Snow?"

"We do get snow early, but no, that's snow. It's salt."

"Salt?"

Atticus nodded. "Salt plains. And some of those lakes aren't lakes but sinkholes. It's surprisingly sandy around Fort Little Buffalo."

"I have never seen a sinkhole."

"Well, if you get the chance, before the weather closes the roads down, head south, back into Alberta, and find Pine Lake. It's a series of sinkholes, and it's one of the most beautiful, serene places. If it was still summer, I would suggest it as a good spot to swim. The river is too dangerous to swim in with the rapids."

"I'm afraid I'm going to miss swimming weather, then. I should be back in Calgary by next summer."

Atticus didn't say anything else. And another awkward silence fell between them. She knew that the hospital in Fort Little Buffalo wanted her to stay.She may be doing a maternity leave, but they were always hungry for more qualified doctors here. They had offered that right away, but she turned them down. Penny was beginning to understand that it was hard to keep doctors in the north, but her home hospital was Calgary. When she went back, she was going with her head held high.

She didn't say anything else for the rest of their forty-minute flight.

Which turned out to be the longest forty minutes of her life.

She was very thankful to see Hay River on the horizon and hear Atticus communicate with the tower in order to land.

She just wanted to get to the hospital. Pick up the supplies they needed and fly back to Fort Little Buffalo to get this six months over and done with as quickly as possible.

CHAPTER THREE

PENNY TRAILED BEHIND Atticus into the Hay River Hospital. She just followed his lead because he knew everyone and she knew no one. They hadn't said much to each other on the short truck ride to the hospital. As much as she wished she could talk to him about work, he had made it clear on their first meeting that he wasn't pleased that she was an admirer of his work. Which seemed contradictory to all other surgeons of his caliber that she'd met.

Especially Walter.

Yet there wasn't any more they could talk about, because Penny refused to be sucked into any kind of relationship other than professional.

Her phone buzzed. She groaned, glancing at it. It was Walter.

Atticus stopped and turned. "Calgary again? Don't they realize you work here now?"

"No," Penny grumbled, then sighed. "Patients are important."

"So are the ones here," he said sternly.

"I know. I'm focused on this. I am. I did consult on the case…"

Atticus nodded curtly. "You need to shut those notifications off."

"You're right." She silenced her phone. "I have

a hard time separating from my work in Calgary. I'm sorry."

A strange look crossed his face. "You're needed here. Remember that."

Warmth spread across her cheeks and she nodded, feeling slightly chastised. "I know."

He nodded again and walked toward an older woman who was headed in their direction.

"I'm Dr. Bush." The immunologist smiled and shook their hands. "Dr. Spike, a pleasure."

Atticus grunted in response. Clearly it wasn't that much of a pleasure.

"I'm Dr. Burman," Penny said, sidestepping Atticus. "I'm so glad you're able to give me what I need. The patient flew in from a remote village."

Dr. Bush shrugged. "It's no problem. I'm thrilled that someone who is able to do the testing can. I only get to Fort Little Buffalo once every three months, and I just did a stint there. I'm only here for a couple of weeks before I head up to Yellowknife and then Inuvik."

"Where is your home hospital?" Penny asked, confused.

Dr. Bush sighed, "I don't really have a set one. I live in Yellowknife, but I like traveling around to the other hospitals. These smaller hospitals can't really keep the staff. If you both follow me to my office, I have everything you need for the testing."

Penny followed Dr. Bush, and Atticus trailed behind.

Hay River was larger than Fort Little Buffalo, but it still was small compared to the hospitals down south. It made sense to her why so many residents of the territories came down to Alberta and went further afield. There wasn't the infrastructure here to support their medical needs.

Dr. Bush opened the door to her office. "Here's everything you need. I hope that will be helpful, and please be sure to give the patient my card. I included it in the package. I do take flights around to some of the more remote villages, and I will be sure to make a trip in the next year to check on him."

"Thank you," Penny said. She lifted the box of supplies, but Atticus took the box from her.

"We'd better go," Atticus said.

Penny frowned at Atticus's impatience and then turned back to Dr. Bush. "I will pass on your information. Thank you, Dr. Bush."

Dr. Bush nodded.

"Thank you, Kylie," Atticus said gruffly and then left her office.

Penny followed him. He was walking quickly through the halls.

"Hey, hold on, what is your rush?" Penny asked.

"This isn't some social call," Atticus said. "This is a visit to get supplies. We have the supplies, and we need to get back."

"Are you like this to all the other physicians in the north?" Penny demanded.

"Like what?" Atticus asked, cocking an eyebrow.

"You are a bit obtuse."

He chuckled. "Obtuse, eh?"

"You're not very social. Dr. Bush went out of her way to help us…"

Atticus paused. "If she wanted to help, she'd set up a proper practice and stay put. She wouldn't fly from location to location for just a week or two at a time."

"Not everyone can stay in the north," she said.

"What you mean is that not everyone wants to stay in the north."

"You practiced in Boston," she snapped.

He frowned and then paused, shifting the box in his arms. "I'm from Fort Little Buffalo."

"You still left it."

His eyes narrowed, and she got the distinct feeling she'd overstepped a boundary. "Fine. You're right. I did, but I came back and I stayed put. People know where to find me."

"Do they? Because five years ago, you sort of disappeared off the map."

A tight smile crossed his face. "Off the map, you say?"

"Yes."

"Good." He marched outside and shouted over his shoulder, "Come on, Dr. Burman, while I'm still young."

Penny stood there fuming. He was insufferable. He might be sexy, and she was highly attracted to him physically, but he really was a pain in her side.

She couldn't figure him out. She thought she was fairly good at figuring people out.

Of course, that was before she met Walter and he completely duped her. So right now, she didn't know what to think or feel or believe. When she and Atticus had talked about the name of his plane, she thought he'd been warming up.

She'd been wrong.

Atticus ran too hot and cold, and she didn't need this in her life.

This was her chance to refocus. To heal so she could go back to Calgary stronger than ever.

Except she was drawn to him. He seemed as lost as she was, and that frustrated her all the more.

All she wanted to do was get back to Fort Little Buffalo and put this whole plane trip behind her.

Atticus really did like Dr. Bush, but they had an understanding. Kylie knew that he liked to keep a low profile. Penny didn't, and he knew that she was trying to figure him out.

It was kind of amusing to him to keep her guessing.

Maybe he was a jerk face, like he had heard ' mumble beneath her breath once. If that was was only for his protection.

Sasha and his friends and colleagues h so warm. He'd felt like they were famil' was so far away from his home.

Then, one mistake, one that wa'

fault and that family, the woman he loved, all turned on him.

Not only was he left with heartache from having a child die under his watch, but he was left alone. There was no one to help him. He'd learned to cope on his own.

He could only rely on himself.

He could trust himself.

The fact that he was enjoying himself with Penny was a huge red flashing light. He didn't want to enjoy too much time with her. If he did, he was putting his heart in danger.

He'd been betrayed once before, and one time was more than enough for him…

"I'm going back to Fort Little Buffalo," he said. "Will you come with me, Sasha?"

"Are you serious?" she asked, disgusted. "Where is that even located?"

"Southern Northwest Territories."

"You mean the wilderness," she quipped sarcastically, but it wasn't a joke. There was a hint of malice in her voice.

"My practice took a hit; the hospital doesn't faith in me. Friends I thought were friends er return my calls. All for something in the g room I couldn't control."

vinced. "It was a high-profile case."

as a risk. Everyone knew that. Fort doesn't care about it, and I'm going to a place where people value medicine over fame. I want you to come with me. I love you, and we're going to get married."

Sasha frowned. Her once sparkling blue eyes were cold. "No. I'm not going with you, and as for our wedding... I think we need to put a pause on that."

"Put a pause on that?" he asked, confused.

"Until things die down. See, I still have a great practice here. I don't make mistakes."

It was like a slap to his face. "I didn't make a mistake. The autopsy cleared me."

"Sure, but the world thinks you made a mistake."

It was obvious to him then. "You were only with me because it looked good on paper. Weren't you?"

Sasha looked away, but he had the answer he needed.

Atticus shook the memory away. He set the supplies carefully in the back seat and then opened the passenger door for Penny.

"Thanks," she said, sliding in.

She might think he was a grump, but he was still a gentleman.

There was a part of him that was whispering in his heart that he could be her friend. Nothing had to happen between them, and his existence in Fort Little Buffalo since he returned home had been lonely and isolating. His sister and her family were close by, but it wasn't the same as his own wife and children.

He had Horatio, but he'd kept everyone else at an arm's length since he came home.

Did he really have to? He could protect his heart, but he could still have friendships, couldn't he?

No. He couldn't.

He could be professional with her. That's it.

"I'm sorry for being antisocial," he said as he drove the truck back to the airport.

Penny's dark eyes widened. "You are something."

"What?" he asked, confused.

"I never know whether I'm coming or going with you."

"And I'm apologizing for that. It's just…it's a protection thing. Usually people want to become my friend because of what I can give them."

Penny's expression softened. "I'm not someone like that. I'm very well-versed in users and emotional vampires."

He felt a pang of pain on her behalf.

He knew all about that.

"Oh?"

"My father was one," she said stonily. Her spine stiffened. "I am not like that, Dr. Spike."

"Atticus," he said.

Pink tinged her high cheeks. And for one quick moment, he wanted to brush his knuckles across her soft skin and comfort her.

"Atticus, then." She almost whispered his name, and it sent a jolt of electricity through him. There was a brief flash of an image, how he imagined he would make her scream his name. It surprised him that such a vivid fantasy hit him merely with his name on her lips.

He cleared his throat and nodded. "I'm sorry for being such a pain since you arrived, but if you know what it's like to be used for something you have and then tossed, you can see my trepidation. This is my home. My work. I won't have it sabotaged."

"I do. Look, I won't lie. I am thrilled to be working with you. It's the one perk of having to leave Calgary and come up here."

"Why did you come up here?"

Penny worried her bottom lip, and he could tell that he had touched a nerve. "Let's just say that everyone makes mistakes, and I put my trust in the wrong person too."

Atticus wanted to ask her more, but as he pulled into the private section of the airport where his plane was housed, he was waved down by one of the air traffic controllers he knew well. Atticus parked the truck and rolled down the driver's side window.

"Atticus," Chuck said.

"What's up?" Atticus asked.

"Everything's been shut down. Fog in Fort Little

Buffalo. Rolled in thick." Chuck held up his phone to show him the radar.

Atticus's stomach knotted. "Fog?"

"It's weird. It was rolling in from the southeast. Weather on Lake Athabasca, and it just settled down in Fort Little Buffalo and Wood Buffalo. All flights south and east have been delayed. We'll call you when you can fly. I suggest you go get some dinner."

Atticus groaned inwardly. "Thanks, Chuck. You have my number."

Chuck nodded and stepped back.

Atticus started the truck, rolled up his window and made a three-point turn to head back to town.

Great.

Being trapped here in Hay River was not putting the distance he wanted between him and Penny.

"We're stuck here?" Penny asked, panic rising in her voice.

"Only until the fog lifts," Atticus said. "Don't worry. I have no doubt we'll get back to Fort Little Buffalo tonight."

"Are you okay to fly at night?"

"I'm not an old man," he teased, gently. "I can see at night."

A smile quirked on her lips. "That's not what I mean…"

"I can fly at night. I don't like it, and the view isn't as pretty, but once we get the all-clear to fly, we can go. Is there anything in particular you feel like eating?"

"No. I'm pretty easygoing, except beef."

"Religious?" he asked, genuinely curious.

"My mother is Hindu. She's not strict, but my grandparents are, and I like to follow their practices. It keeps me connected to my culture."

"Connection to culture is important," he agreed, trying to think of a great place he could take her. Options were limited in Hay River. "I am relearning my own, because when I was a foolish teen, I sort of abandoned it, or rather didn't have much of an interest in it."

"And what is that, if you don't mind me asking?"

"Métis" Atticus responded, heading back out onto the main road. "My father made a living trapping fur, like his ancestors, but he was raised in the city. My grandparents moved him away from their home in the northwest to avoid things like residential school and the sixties scoops. They hid in plain sight the best they could, but when my dad turned twenty, he wanted to reconnect to his Indigenous roots and moved back."

"Are your parents still in Fort Little Buffalo?" Penny asked.

"Yellowknife now," Atticus said. "Dad needs some complex medical care, and they were tired of traveling back and forth. I live in the cabin now."

"You live in a cabin?" Penny asked.

"Why do you sound shocked?"

"I guess I'm always surprised about people choosing to live in cabins. Although the first time I saw you, I got the serious mountain lumberjack vibes."

Atticus snorted. "So, these mountain lumberjack types live in cabins, and surgeons don't?"

Penny laughed softly. "My apologies. Cabin life for you, then?"

"Yes. I'm not that far out of town, but I like the privacy it affords me." He parked in front of small diner that he knew served fresh fish from Great Slave Lake and the Hay River. It was a great place to kill some time until the fog lifted and they could fly back.

"Sally's?" Penny asked.

Atticus nodded. "They cook a mean char here."

"I do like arctic char," Penny said, and then she smiled. "What have I got to lose?"

Atticus grinned. "Time."

He opened the door for her. She walked past him, and he caught the scent of lilac. It was subtle, but it reminded him of summer. It made him want to drink in her scent, and he couldn't help but wonder what her lips tasted like.

How soft they were.

He had to get a hold of these runaway emotions. There was no room in his heart for such foolish notions. His heart was closed.

* * *

Penny had been annoyed that fog was delaying them, and she was a bit uneasy about having dinner with Atticus, but in this situation she was kind of powerless. She could control a lot of things in her life, but not the weather.

More was the pity.

At least she could have a nice piece of arctic char, and she was hungry.

The moment they walked into the diner, which looked like a bit of a dive from the outside, she was hit with the yummy smells of good food. Her stomach grumbled in appreciation. She followed Atticus to a corner booth that was tucked out of the way.

It struck her how much he seemed to enjoy hiding.

Trailing after her in the larger hospital, the cabin in the woods, hiking the less known trails with Horatio and flying his own plane. Now, selecting the farthest table away from the hustle and bustle of everyone else.

He had mentioned being used and betrayed. Penny couldn't help but wonder if that's what happened to him in Boston. The failed surgery of those conjoined twins was heartbreaking, but it wasn't his fault. It was a risky surgery. And the parents were well-known.

Penny had just been fresh out of her internship, and she'd read everything she could about it. Atticus had been taking a risk, but that's what medicine was all about.

If it was her, it would haunt her for sure.

Aren't you haunted?

She'd shut off her notifications, but that didn't stop Walter from emailing and not always about patients.

"So tell me about the case this surgeon is emailing you about," Atticus said.

"Cardio case. Atrial septal deviation."

Atticus cocked an eyebrow. "Shouldn't they consult with the cardiothoracic surgeon in Calgary?"

"I won't take that as an insult," she teased.

"It's not, but you're here," Atticus stated. "I have no doubt you're brilliant, but you're far away."

"I consulted on this before. Just trying to tie up loose ends."

That's all he needed to know.

He didn't need to know she was here to prove herself to Calgary.

That was her burden to bear.

"Good evening, folks," the waiter said, coming up with two menus. "Our special tonight is char, rice and broccoli. We also have a Saskatoon berry crumble. It'll be the last of the year, so my suggestion is to get it while you can."

"That sounds good," Penny said brightly, not having to look at the menu. "I'll have the char special and the crumble. Can I get some tea?"

The waiter nodded and looked at Atticus.

"I'll have the same special, just water for me though," Atticus said, not meeting the waiter's eye.

"Awesome." The waiter collected the menus and left them alone.

"I've never had a Saskatoon berry," Penny said, trying to make conversation to break the uncomfortable silence between them.

Atticus smiled, but only briefly. "Aren't you from Alberta?"

"I am."

"They're all over western Canada."

"I know, but I just haven't had one. I have had huckleberries. My grandpa would take me for a walk in the foothills, and we would pick them."

"Huckleberries are the best. If you like huckleberries, you'll like Saskatoon berries. I swear."

"I'll hold you to that promise," she teased. "So, tell me about this cabin."

"Really?"

"Sure," she said. "I can tell you that I live in a double-wide trailer that I rent from one of the locals, who refers to it as a guest house."

"Modular homes are popular up here. Easy to build when there's permafrost, rock and sand."

"You're avoiding my question."

Atticus pursed his lips together. "I suppose I am. There's not much to tell. I believe my paternal great-grandfather built it. He was a German immigrant, and he came out to the northwest. Escaping something. He met my paternal great-grandmother, who was Métis and Dene. They built it. It was tucked away. He protected her and their children from residential school. They lived off the land. Then it passed down to my father eventually. And now it's mine. My sister had no desire to be involved with it."

"You have a sister?" Penny asked. "Does she live in Fort Little Buffalo?"

He nodded. "She does. She has three girls. My nieces. One is sixteen, one is thirteen, and the other is nine, almost ten. All three years apart. They love Horatio. Me they can take or leave most days. Teen girls…"

Penny smiled. "It's nice to have nieces. It was just me and my mom, unless you count my half siblings. My older half brother has children, but I've never met them."

"Do you have any other half siblings?" Atticus asked.

"One. A sister." Penny smiled. "She's studying neuroscience in Calgary. She visits me when she gets a chance. Much to our brother Raj's chagrin."

"Why would Raj have a problem with that?"

Penny sighed. "Raj blames me and my mother for our father's infidelity. Although my mother had no idea the man she fell in love with had a wife in India that he was waiting to bring over to Canada. She thought they would get married, but instead he left us for them. My little sister was born about six years after my father left us in Canada. She sought me out when she first came to Calgary, and we formed a relationship. She's a joy."

"Families can be so tricky."

"They can." She tried to shake the sadness that was clouding her heart at that moment. She longed for a family. As much as she loved the family she did have, she longed for closeness and connection with both her siblings. She didn't want to think about her father or Raj or any of that. She didn't want to think of the many nights she'd heard her mother cry herself to sleep after being betrayed.

A pain Penny knew all too well.

She was just glad there were no children involved.

Penny had always wanted her own children, not that she saw that happening, but if she did ever get the chance to be so blessed with her most secret dream of having a family, a loving husband to share her life with, she was going to make sure that they didn't feel the kind of pain she felt when her father left her.

And even after all this time, she could still feel the acute burn, the sting of tears as they ran down her face, watching her father drive away and having her whole world shattered. So, as much as she wanted kids, how could she trust someone enough to make that happen?

The waiter returned with their drinks. A water for Atticus and a small stainless steel teapot, a tea bag and a mug. Not the fanciest, but it would do just fine.

"Your dinner will be ready shortly," the waiter said.

"Thank you," Penny said as Atticus nodded, acknowledging the waiter. The waiter left. She poured the hot water over her tea bag in the cup. The tea gave her a warm, cozy feeling, which she appreciated as she heard an early autumn rainstorm start, the pattering a gentle sound on the metal roof of the diner.

"I hope this rain won't delay us," Penny said offhandedly.

"Shouldn't," Atticus stated. "I've been watching the radar. I'm anxious to get back to Fort Little Buffalo too."

"Why? Because you can't stand being alone with me?" she asked, feeling slightly unwanted. Maybe even kind of a burden.

"Something like that," he said huskily, and then he smiled ever so slightly. It caught her off guard. The way he said that caused a tingle to run through her, and she met his gaze across the table.

He was so handsome, and she was angry at herself for being attracted to him.

"In all truth, I was worried about getting back to Horatio, but I have texted my eldest niece, and she'll make sure that goon has a walk."

"He is adorable."

"So I've been told," he muttered. "He needs a bit more training. He's only been with me for a year."

"He's a rescue, right?" she asked.

"He was part of a sled team. Someone who needed a good team of working dogs bred him, and they were training for the Iditarod, but Horatio had hip dysplasia. He required a FHO surgery."

"FHO?" she asked. "I'm not sure what that is. I'm not up-to-date on veterinary medicine."

He smiled softly. "It's where they remove the ball at the top of the femur after a dislocation, usually from hip dysplasia. A false joint forms, but it shortens the dog's leg. Sometimes you can see that one of Horatio's hind legs doesn't touch the ground."

"Really?"

Atticus nodded. "Long story short, the owner had no use for him and couldn't afford the surgery. Instead of the owner putting him down, I took him on. He had the surgery, and I had to keep him quiet for several months while he healed. Which was a challenge, but he was always a bit of a reckless sled dog. Never really liked to listen. So, he needs some work."

Penny smiled. "That's sweet."

"Perhaps, but such an undertaking. Still, Horatio is my buddy. I didn't realize how lonely I had…" He trailed off and cleared his throat. "Anyway, Horatio loves my niece, and she can watch him until we get back to Fort Little Buffalo."

The waiter returned and brought them their dinner. It smelled delicious. All talk ended of loneliness and those uncomfortable conversations that veered too close to their personal lives. She enjoyed her arctic char and glanced out the window at the gentle autumn rain and darkness creeping in as the sun set.

Penny understood that feeling of loneliness.

She had felt it keenly since she was small. Her father left when she was five, and she would see him sporadically when it suited him. When she made him happy, which wasn't often.

And she longed for more.

She longed for things that she was pretty sure were far out of her grasp.

CHAPTER FOUR

AFTER THEIR DINNER and dessert, Penny paid for the bill because Atticus was the one who flew them there. He tried to pay his way, but she refused.

She was strong.

Independent.

Stubborn. And he liked that.

During the Saskatoon berry crumble portion of their dinner, they got a call that the fog had lifted from Fort Little Buffalo, and the rain had ended. It was okay to travel back.

Atticus got them to the airport. He parked his friend's truck back in the hangar, and they got their supplies loaded. He was impressed that he could give Penny instructions on how to help him ready the plane.

She didn't complain or question anything.

She just got to work. Soon they were boarded, and he was contacting the tower for takeoff. He made his checks, and Penny was more comfortable this time sitting beside him, with her ridiculously big earphones on.

He brought his plane out to the runway and began his taxiing for takeoff. The sky was clear, with only a few dark clouds in the sky. Stars were coming out, but Penny gasped as they climbed up.

"Is everything okay?" he asked.

"The sky…"

"Yeah?" He was confused.

"The stars… I haven't seen them like this since I was a little girl."

He smiled reluctantly; her eyes were wide in wonder.

"They'll get more brilliant the later it gets. And tonight is a good night for the aurora."

"Oh," she gasped. "I hope we see it. It's been so long since I've seen that too. In the city, you don't see it much, or rather not at all with all the lights."

"Light pollution ruins so much," he agreed. The aurora was something that he'd taken for granted for a long time and really didn't learn to appreciate until he came back home to mend his broken heart.

When he was younger, he didn't appreciate his roots. He didn't want to stay here. He went to university in Toronto, enraptured with the city and the nightlife. Then Boston came calling, and he was trained under some of the most prominent pediatricians and neonatologists. He had talent.

He had been charming back then, because he was just so happy to put the north out of his mind, and he did love the twinkling lights of the city.

Until it lost its appeal.

Though it wasn't the city, but the people, that had ruined it all for him.

When he'd come back to Fort Little Buffalo, his sister Ginny had been there, waiting for him. The hospital, the people appreciated him. It took him a long time to see that, and then his eyes were opened when the aurora came out.

It spoke to him, in its many varying colors of greens, and he knew that he had been duped by something that wasn't real. Fame wasn't what mattered.

All that mattered was saving lives.

And he was doing just that. Although there were parts of him that were lonely and longed for more.

Children.

A family of his own, like his sister Ginny had.

He glanced over at Penny, and his heart skipped a beat as he watched her, smiling in the dim light of the cockpit. Her joyous face was illuminated only by the lights that his plane cast. She was so beautiful. He was still taken aback at how attracted to her he'd been when he first saw her.

Atticus never really took stock in that old idea of love at first sight, and he didn't love her, but he'd certainly been hit with a bolt of lightning when he saw her. When he was around her, all he could think about doing was kissing her, protecting her. He just wanted to hold her in his arms and drink her in.

And she was proving herself to be smart, witty and strong.

She didn't shy away. She didn't back down.

He liked that about her.

And how much will she hurt you when she leaves? a little voice asked inside his head.

The little voice was his logic, reminding him of the pain he'd felt when Sasha wouldn't come to Canada with him. When she'd turned her back on him and moved on so quickly after he left. He'd promised himself he would never be that foolish again.

"Oh, wow!" Penny gasped.

He looked up to see the aurora quiver and appear in front of them. It was faint, but it was there. A ribbon of light, all thanks to the atmosphere and the rays from the sun.

He smiled, his heart warming, watching her excitement. He wanted to share her awe and wonder. He wanted to pull her close, and his blood heated thinking about all the other things he wished he could do with her.

And he couldn't let himself think like that.

She was off limits. Even if there was a part of him, one that he'd thought dead and buried, that didn't want her to be off limits.

"Fort Little Buffalo is just there. We'll be back soon," he said gruffly.

"Oh, good," she said stiffly. "I want to check in on my patient. I'll spare him the allergy test until the morning. It won't take long to get results."

Atticus just nodded as he focused on the lights of the runway.

It was going to be hard to keep his distance for

the next six months while she worked in Fort Little Buffalo. It wasn't a big town, and the hospital wasn't big, either.

But for the sake of his heart, he was certainly going to try.

Penny hadn't slept much the night before. The first night she'd come to Fort Little Buffalo, she didn't sleep because she was worried about her job. Now she couldn't sleep because all she could think about was Atticus.

He was infuriating, but she saw a different side to him. A side that she wanted to get to know, and she was treading into dangerous territory as far as her heart was concerned. The only reason she was here was to work.

She wasn't here to make connections.

Still, there had been a few moments when they had shared something. And there had been a few moments when she was sure he'd wanted to tell her more, but had held himself back. There were times she would look up and see him smiling at her, just a half smile under that neatly trimmed beard and his dark eyes twinkling at her.

It made her heart beat just a bit faster and her body zing with anticipation.

Every time she closed her eyes, she could see him. She ended up tossing and turning all night.

Her phone rang and she cringed, hoping it wasn't Walter.

There had been times, before she knew he was married, when she'd thought she was falling in love, and she'd be excited to get a call from him. Now, not so much.

She looked at her phone and let out a sigh of relief.

"Hi, Mom!"

"Penny, you haven't called me in a couple of days… I thought you might've been eaten by a bear."

Penny chuckled. "No, mom. The bear would choke on me. I'm too stubborn."

Her mother laughed. "I know you get busy, so I thought I'd call now. I still don't really understand why you left Calgary for the Northwest Territories."

Penny worried her bottom lip. "Opportunity."

"Opportunity?"

"Yes. There's a surgeon here I've admired for some time, and I'm working with him."

"Oh. Good. Well, I'm glad you're not eaten. Call me soon."

"Yes, Mom. I love you. Tell Grandma I love her too." Penny ended the call.

She decided to go for a run, only this time she would avoid the path where she'd had her first run-in with Horatio and Atticus. She would stick to the streets in town and maybe get a cup of tea or coffee afterwards.

Outside there was frost coating everything with

a distinct bite in the air. Calgary was no stranger to cold weather and longer winters, but it was only September, and she wasn't quite prepared to feel the sting of winter.

As she ran, she thought of how she could avoid Atticus, other than communicating what was needed for work.

She had to make sure that their relationship remained a professional one. That's all.

There was no need for friendship when her time here was finite.

Then what was your excuse in Calgary?

In the past she had given the excuse of time, which was true. She didn't have a lot of time for anything outside of work, and she was still trying to figure out how Walter had wiggled his way into her life.

The one time she'd let someone through her carefully constructed barriers, and look how that turned out.

Penny shook her head. She hated that her brain was going over and over this again. She didn't want that. When she ran, she would turn her mind to work, to her patients. Running was a way to clear her head and to muddle through the problems she had to overcome to save someone's life, it wasn't a time to muddle through her personal problems.

There was never a good time for that.

As she rounded the corner, there was a shout and

some wild barking. A huge furry behemoth of a dog jumped up in front of her.

Penny stumbled, but righted herself, leaning over with her hands on her knees to catch her breath. She glanced up and saw that familiar face.

"Horatio," she muttered.

The dog, panting, seemed to be smiling. He cocked his head, and his tail was wagging a mile a minute. He seemed thrilled that she remembered his name.

"Horatio!" Atticus came running down the street, holding a dog doo bag.

"I see your friend distracted you by making you scoop up his offerings before he bolted," Penny mused, straightening up.

Atticus sighed and glanced down at the bag. "Yeah, something like that."

"What're you doing here? I thought you walked him at the park near the town sign."

"You jog there and I didn't want to interrupt you, so I decided the river run was better."

Penny sighed and smiled. "I thought the same thing. Besides, I heard the hill down to the rapids is quite steep."

"It is," Atticus admitted. "It tires Horatio out, but it's a bit of a chore to keep him out of the water. There're dangerous rapids."

"Yeah, he doesn't seem to listen to you much," she mumbled, reaching down to rub Horatio's head.

Atticus disposed of Horatio's refuse in a nearby

garbage bin, then sanitized his hands with some gel from his pockets. "So it would seem. He likes you, though."

"Apparently." She glanced down at Horatio. "Are we meant to be friends?"

Horatio held up a paw, his ears back. It melted her heart a bit. She could never resist a dog. She had always been partial to them. Just had no time for them.

No time for anything really.

Not when work was her life.

Right here, in this moment, she could afford to have some much-needed stress release stroking the head of a very naughty sled dog.

"Do you mind if I come in and watch you administer the allergy test?" Atticus asked, which bothered her.

"You want to watch me give an allergy test to my patient?" she asked, feeling a little annoyed.

It's because he doesn't think you'll do it right.

"Yes. I think that was apparent when I asked the question." There were hints of amusement and confusion in his voice.

"I have no problem. I guess I'm just surprised."

"Why?" he asked.

"I figured it's just a routine test and you're…"

"Atticus Spike," he said tensely. "Look, I was never overly interested in allergies, but as you said, there is no allergist in this hospital, and we had to fly to Hay River to get what we needed. I would like to observe and possibly learn. So that when you leave, I can run the tests if needed."

She was surprised.

No one ever wanted her to teach them anything.

Maybe she was wrong about judging his intentions too quickly.

"You mean I get to teach the great physician Atticus Spike something?"

He rolled his eyes and smiled slightly. "I suppose so."

"I guess that can be accommodated."

"Thanks."

There was laughter, and they both turned to see a small group of people walking up from the river. Her eyes immediately tracked to the straggler of the group. He was a few paces behind and seemed to be sweating profusely even though it was chilly out.

He wasn't a particularly large man, but he was struggling to catch up and was grabbing at his arm.

Penny jogged past the group to him. "Sir? Are you well?"

"Fine," he wheezed, but the closer Penny got to him, she could tell that he wasn't okay. "The hill."

"It's steep," Penny agreed, falling in step beside him. "Why don't you rest?"

"No." He shook his head. "I did this hike ten years ago. I can...." The man trailed off, and his knees buckled as he fell down on them and then facedown into the sandy path.

"Sir!" Penny called out. Then she looked up to see that his group had paused, and Atticus was tying Horatio to a lamppost before running to her side.

"Call emergency services," Atticus shouted over his shoulder to the man's friends.

"Help me roll him over," Penny said.

Atticus helped rolled the unconscious man onto his back. He was pale, and his pulse was thready.

"Sir," Penny called out as she quickly made an assessment of his vitals, checking his eyes and his throat and his breathing. There was a reaction still in his pupils, and he wasn't breathing.

It could be anything from a heart attack to a stroke to something like an aortic rupture. She wasn't sure, but she could give him CPR. Atticus was a step ahead of her as he was undoing the man's light jacket, his hands poised over the man's sternum.

"Blow when I say," Atticus told her.

"I know what to do." Penny tilted the man's head back, waiting for when she could administer a breath. She most often had to preform CPR on pediatric patients and not adults, so she had to remind herself of that.

She watched as Atticus pumped, counting in her head.

He stopped, and she bent over and administered a breath. Atticus started compressions again. She watched his strong forearms working the man's chest, trying to get the heart to start again.

When he stopped, she leaned over and administered a breath.

The man coughed, breathing on his own, but he was groggy and was still not very conscious.

The ambulance siren pierced the silence of the forest as it rounded the bend.

"It's a good thing he passed out where he did," Atticus said. "It would be harder to get to him had he collapsed down the trail at the rocks. The ambulance can get here."

Penny nodded in answer, but she didn't know.

She hadn't made it down the trail, and she doubted that she would be heading there today.

The ambulance parked close to them, and the paramedics jumped out.

"Atticus," one of the male paramedics acknowledged as he opened the back door to pull out the gurney.

"Hey, Josh." Atticus stood up and went over to let the paramedics know what happened.

Penny got up as the paramedics knelt down beside her patient. She motioned for his companions to come over, and she took a step back to let the paramedics do their job.

Atticus stood beside her. "The RCMP are coming by the hospital later to talk to us."

"Why?" Penny asked.

"They just want find out what happened. He's

not from here, he's from Ontario, so they like to cover all their bases, plus for insurance reasons."

"Are they taking him to Fort Little Buffalo?"

"For now, but they'll most likely airlift him to Yellowknife or Edmonton."

"I'm glad we were both here when it happened," she said.

Atticus glanced over at her. There was a brief flicker of a smile, but only just. He nodded in response. Never did she think her first case with Dr. Atticus Spike would be just administering CPR to an adult, in the middle of a trail, in the woods.

When she pictured practicing medicine with other physicians she admired, it was always something more challenging in the field of pediatric medicine. Still, them being here today had saved that man's life. Or at least for now.

Horatio barked as the paramedics loaded up their patient. Atticus turned and looked back. "I better get him home."

"Yes, and I need a shower before my shift."

They both walked back to Horatio, who was patiently waiting for them, his ears up and his tail wagging a mile a minute. Atticus untied his leash, and Penny gave her furry friend a pat on the head.

"When are you administering the test?" Atticus asked.

"As soon as I get there. So, in about two hours? You still want to come?"

"I do. It'll be nice to see you in action. And what I mean is, at the hospital."

She laughed nervously. "I get it."

"Okay, well, I'll see you in a couple hours then." Atticus gave a sharp command to Horatio, who followed with a reluctant look back at her.

Penny sighed and stepped back as the sirens came on, and she watched the ambulance make its way up the sandy path to the hospital.

She waited until it was gone and then turned back the way she'd come to get ready for a day of work. Her master plan of avoiding Atticus had failed, so she had to mentally prepare herself to be in close proximity to a man who both annoyed and excited her, for an entire day.

Part of her was dreading it, but the other part, the one she wanted to ignore, was secretly thrilled. And that secret thrill unnerved her.

CHAPTER FIVE

ATTICUS DIDN'T KNOW what possessed him to want to watch Penny administer the allergy test. He was honest with her; allergy testing had never been a skill set that he'd really pursued when he was going through medical school.

He was always interested in pediatric medicine.

He'd had another sister, his twin, who had passed away when they were seventeen after complications from an illness she had struggled with her whole life. When Andrea died, he decided then and there to pull up his grades and work his tail off to get into university and then into medical school.

His focus had been pediatric medicine and then neonatology when his eldest niece had been premature. His eldest niece reminded him so much of Andrea, even right down to her name. Atticus wanted to heal children. His problem, though, was that he'd lost sight of the real reasons and got so caught up with success and fame in Boston that he didn't see all the wolves in sheep's clothing that were surrounding him and using him.

When he got back to Fort Little Buffalo and was able to practice on kids like his late sister, that's when he could see the difference he was making, and he learned to love medicine again. He was disappointed at himself for not having the skill of performing a simple allergy test.

And not learning how to properly do that when he had been in Boston. He had been so focused on specializing back then.

If he learned now, he might convince the board to stock the supplies, and then see if he could open a clinic, run through the hospital, to administer the tests for the surrounding area.

Maybe then they could attract specialists, instead of Dr. Bush just coming by every quarter. He was thankful they had that locum physician, but it wasn't enough. He wanted to do more for this community. A community that didn't care about his reputation or his fame.

This community was his home. He might not be social, but he did belong here.

He was humble enough to learn from another doctor who didn't have as many years of practice as he had. Atticus knew a lot of other physicians who wouldn't learn.

They stagnated in their arrogance.

Penny was smart and confident, but there was no arrogance there.

If anything, there was a bit of vulnerability that she was hiding. For example, that Calgary doctor's texts seemed to weigh heavy on her. He would hate to think she was being used. She didn't deserve that.

She was a doctor of worth.

After he made sure that Horatio was settled back at home, he had a quick shower and got ready for the day. For the first time in a long time, he was actually excited to go to work. He loved his job, but he was really looking forward to it because he could work with her. His stomach was in knots, and he found it impossible to eat anything other than a bite of toast then finished off his coffee that had gone cold.

When he got to the hospital, he found out from the administrative staff on the pediatric floor that Penny was in her office, getting everything ready to administer the test to her patient.

Atticus dropped off his stuff in his office and made his way down the hall to the office that was used for temporary doctors. It had no windows and was tucked in the corner, with Penny's name taped to the front of the door.

His heart skipped a beat and he cleared his throat, trying to calm his nerves. He didn't understand why he was so jittery, and he was annoyed by it.

He was better than this.

He knocked on the door.

"Come in," Penny called out in that lovely singsong voice she had. He had noticed that yesterday when they had been talking over dinner, how sweet her voice sounded. How poised she was, but she wasn't a pushover.

Which was why he was drawn to her all the more.

"Hey, I'm not late, am I?"

"Nope, just getting all the solutions ready." She continued with her work. "It's really a simple procedure. I made sure before I left yesterday that the patient didn't take any antihistamines unless it was absolutely necessary."

"That would invalidate the test?" he asked.

She nodded. "Yes, it wouldn't work. Thankfully, Marcus didn't need anything last night. He was stable, and he's ready for this test."

"Have you heard from respirology yet?" Atticus asked.

Penny shook her head. "Not yet. They were inundated yesterday with some pneumonia patients and a case of tuberculosis?"

"Why the question about the tuberculosis?" Atticus asked.

"I don't think that I've ever seen a case of TB in Canada."

"It exists. Unfortunately, in places that are remote and without access to proper vaccines, it can be common."

"Well, thankfully Marcus has been fully vaccinated," Penny said.

Her phone rang.

Just by glancing at the screen, he could see it was a Calgary number.

It annoyed him she was still so attached to the big-city hospital.

Why was she even here then?

City didn't always equal better.

Penny ignored the phone. "Everything is ready. These are just the airborne allergens. I've had blood drawn and sent to a special lab in Calgary to determine some food sensitivities and other allergies that can't be tested through the skin. I suspect, since he's having issues with breathing, that it's something airborne."

"And you suspect asthma, like the locum doctor?" Atticus asked.

Penny nodded, and they headed out of her office to go to Marcus's room in the next wing. "The perfect environment for him would be the desert. Somewhere dry and hot."

"We don't have humidity like the southern parts of Canada."

"No. That's at least something. I know rationally that not everyone can move to Arizona or somewhere like that."

"I have no desire to move to Arizona," he said dryly.

She cocked an eyebrow. "Oh? Do you have a hate on for Arizona too?"

"What do you mean, too?" Atticus asked, shocked.

"Well, you seem kind of surly about a lot of things," she said sardonically.

He sighed. "I don't hate Arizona. I'm just not a desert badlands type of person. I prefer the woods and the north."

"So I gathered." She smiled at him.

"I like it when you smile," he said, and instantly he regretted telling her that.

A pink blush rose in her cheeks. "When I smile?"

"Yeah, it's preferable to the glares you usually shoot in my direction. Don't think I haven't noticed you giving me the side-eye from time to time."

Penny laughed then. Really laughed out loud, and he found himself laughing too. He couldn't remember the last time he'd laughed like this, with someone else even. It had been a long time, and as he thought back to all those times he had been with Sasha, there hadn't been this kind of laughter.

Sasha and he laughed, but usually it was her laughing over something inane. He'd soon learned it was all fake.

And it just made him even more angry at himself for not seeing it sooner.

"I'm sorry for glaring at you," she said, smiling at him in a way that made his pulse rate go up a notch.

"No, you're not," he grumbled.

"You're right. I'm not, not really. You deserved it that first time we met. You were so annoying."

"Tell you what, how about we start over? This is a new day. We can start fresh and right, so that we can have a good, proper working relationship for the next six months."

"Coworkers." She nodded. "We'll keep it professional."

A chill ran down his spine when she said that, because it reminded him that her time here was finite, but he shook that feeling of unhappiness away. He didn't understand why it had bubbled up just then. He didn't know her. There was no reason to feel that way, and he didn't want to.

"Right. Professional and courteous. We'll shake on it."

Penny took his hand. Her skin was so soft it sent a tendril of longing through him. It confirmed what he'd thought about her the moment he had first laid eyes on her. When he'd imagined what it would feel like to touch her. She pulled her hand away quickly.

"So, shall we get this allergy test over and done with?" she asked, clearing her throat.

"Yes. Let's get this young man some answers."

Penny knocked on the door before heading in with a bright smile on her face for her patient. Atticus followed her in, marveling at her poise, her bubbly personality when it came to her patients.

And for one brief flicker, he wished that her time here wasn't so short.

That she would be here permanently so he could get to know her better. Even if it meant she was a danger to his heart.

Penny finished administering the allergy test. She tested for all airborne allergens. Now they had to wait for fifteen minutes to see if there were any welts that arose. Marcus was already complaining of itching, and she could see a few welts were already rising.

"I'll come back in fifteen and make a note," she said to Marcus's mom.

"Thank you, Dr. Burman," the woman said.

Penny cleaned up the mess with the help of Atticus, who observed the process, and they stepped out of the room to dispose of what they didn't need into the medical waste.

Atticus closed the patient's door as they entered the hall. "That seemed simple enough."

"It's extremely easy to administer. A proper immunologist or allergist would be better to tailor the correct medicines, but I can call a friend in Calgary once I know what Marcus is allergic to."

They disposed of the used gloves and equipment, and Penny made her way to a computer to input the information in Marcus's chart.

"I'd better get to the floor," Atticus said. "I have some rounds to complete. Thank you again for showing me."

Penny smiled, glancing up at him briefly. "It's no problem."

Atticus smiled back at her and then turned to walk away, his hands in the pockets of his white lab coat. She found herself watching him as he walked away. When he smiled at her like that, when he wasn't all closed off to any kind of nice gesture, he was incredibly charming and fun to be around.

There were times when she found it hard to talk

to him because she didn't know what to say. She was fighting back the urge to blush and go weak at the knees around him, but then, she couldn't ever remember wanting to talk to Walter this much.

She couldn't remember having these kinds of swirly feelings about him. She found Walter attractive and smart, but with Atticus, there was something different, and she couldn't quite put her finger on it.

She felt like she did in high school when she'd had a crush on the bad boy of her class. The loner boy, the troublemaker. The boy she'd never really had the guts to talk to because she was a bit of a wallflower and so different from the other girls, because she worked hard in school and was a poor kid.

So she'd kept to herself and kept her teenage crush close to heart, watching him from afar. The thing was, she didn't want that kind of man.

She didn't want the poet bad boy.

That was the kind of man her father had been. The kind of man her mother had fallen for, and look how that turned out. It'd nearly destroyed her mother, and it had shattered Penny's world.

The way things seemed to go in cases of love, she really didn't want anyone.

She didn't need anyone.

Penny tore her gaze away from Atticus's retreating form and continued putting information into Marcus's chart.

"Code blue. Code blue."

Penny's heart stopped, and she glanced up to see the flashing light over the door of Marcus's room.

Oh. God.

She quickly ran for the room as the code team was racing in a crash cart. She sidestepped them and ran to Marcus's bedside. His lips were blue, and he was gasping for air. His mother was crying.

"I don't know what happened," she wailed. "He just said he couldn't breathe, and then he started choking."

Penny leaned over him, opened his mouth and saw his throat was closed. He was swelling. She needed to get a breathing tube down his throat. They needed to intubate him now.

Atticus came into the room. "Status?"

"Swelling in the throat. It appears to be an anaphylactic response to an allergen," Penny responded, placing a mask over Marcus's face and squeezing the Ambu bag to breathe for him. The code team set up monitors, but she needed to get an endotracheal tube into him. Atticus had a central line inserted in him. She knew that Atticus was administering anesthesia and a muscle relaxer.

"I need epinephrine," Atticus stated. "We'll get it into him now."

It would make the process of intubating him much easier.

If that failed, she didn't want to think that far ahead, even though she knew that's often where her brain went. It worked three or four steps ahead of her so she could get a clear picture.

She knew what would have to be done, she just hoped she wouldn't have to do it for this young boy.

Atticus was leaning over, checking Marcus's nose and his eyes for a response.

"I need a five-millimeter tube," Penny ordered. "And this bed dropped."

A nurse handed her what she needed, and she moved to the head of the bed as it lowered. Another nurse took over the Ambu bag. She tilted Marcus's head back and opened his mouth with the laryngoscope.

The throat was closed.

Try as she might, she couldn't get the tube down his throat. It was too far gone.

Dammit.

"Tracheostomy?" Atticus asked.

"I don't have any other option," Penny said.

She glanced up to see Marcus's mother across the room. "Josephine, you need to leave. I need to perform a tracheostomy to help Marcus breathe."

Josephine sobbed and nodded as a nurse escorted her from the room.

Penny got to work. She prepped the area on the boy's throat, feeling where she could make the tracheotomy incision. She hated having to do this to a child, but they had no choice. He needed to breathe. He would die if she didn't.

Atticus was prepping a surgical field. She didn't

even have to ask him. He too knew exactly what needed to be done in this moment.

She made the incision, and Atticus was there by her side, helping her as they opened the airway and inserted the tube so he could breathe. Once everything was secured, his blood pressure returned to normal, and he was breathing.

The epinephrine was working, and his heart stopped racing.

Penny sighed. "I've never seen an anaphylactic reaction happen so fast."

"What caused it?" Atticus asked as he leaned over and checked on their patient, making sure his vitals were stable.

"I didn't stop to look." She turned his arm over and checked for the usual allergens. Nothing was raised on his arm except a couple of scary hives.

Mold.

"What is it?" Atticus asked, noticing her staring at that large welt.

"It's mold," she said. She worried on her bottom lip. "I will need to know where to send a blood test, for a specialty test."

"What blood test are you thinking of?" Atticus asked.

"I need an immunoglobin E antibody test. Mold allergens, especially one that he could be dangerously allergic to, will be in his blood. The immunoglobin E in his blood will be elevated and hopefully highly enough. Also, the family home should be checked for toxins, and he'll need a biopsy of his lungs to see what's growing in there."

"He may not have asthma, then?" Atticus asked.

"He still very well could, but if there's mold, then it just exacerbated the whole thing. Usually, mold happens in humid or wet environments."

"There's flooding up here," Atticus stated.

"Then the home needs to be checked, and I need to have that blood test done. Once his swelling comes down, we can remove the tracheostomy tube."

"Good job, Dr. Burman," Atticus said. There was a look of admiration in his eyes. It sent a thrill through her, because in that moment, she appreciated his validation.

"Thank you," she said. "Now I have to go tell his mother."

"I'll give the orders. You speak to the mother," Atticus said.

Penny removed her gloves and disposed of them. She made her way out into the hall, where Josephine was sitting alone, wringing her hands. Penny met her terrified eyes as she stood.

"Dr. Burman?" she asked. There was a hint of fear in her voice. Understandably so.

"He's stable," Penny said softly. "He appears to be allergic to mold."

"Mold?" Josephine asked. "We had a flood a

couple years ago in the village. Most homes had water damage, but the government came in and cleared everything."

"You need to check yourself. In fact, I can give you a home air test. Marcus may very well have asthma, but it could be caused from this mold. Did his symptoms start shortly after the flood?"

Josephine's eyes widened. "They did."

Penny nodded. "He has an anaphylactic reaction to it. I don't know what kind of mold is specifically in your house, but he reacted with a hive to the most common. I'm worried it might be *Stachybotrys chartarum*, also known as black mold. It's highly toxic."

Josephine's eyes filled with tears. "What happens now?"

"I had to perform a tracheostomy in his throat. Once the swelling goes down, we can remove the tube and close the incision." Penny reached out and rubbed Josephine's shoulder. "I know it's scary, but he'll remain sedated until then. I also want to administer an immunoglobin E antibody test. It'll check for certain proteins in his blood, and I'll write a prescription for EpiPens."

"Thank you, Dr. Burman."

"Try not to worry. We'll find out what's happening."

"My husband is on his way here. He's taking a flight in. He can test the air at home."

Penny nodded and smiled. "We'll make sure he has it. Once we find out what's growing in your home, we can treat it, and that will keep Marcus safe."

"Can I see him?" Josephine asked.

"Of course."

Josephine smiled and headed into her son's room. Atticus slipped out as she came in.

"How is Marcus?" Penny asked.

"Sedated and stable. You suspect black mold?"

Why was he questioning her? It was frustrating.

"I do. It's the most toxic, and Marcus's mother confirmed my suspicion. His symptoms started just after the flood. She mentioned government people came in and declared the homes safe."

Atticus rolled his eyes. "Not a surprise."

"I'm sending her husband, who is on his way here, with a simple air test for mold. We can forward it to a lab and find out what kind of mold. Either way, he can't go home until that's solved. He'll die."

"So he's an inpatient here for now."

"For now," Penny agreed. She rubbed her temples; she had a headache starting, and she realized she hadn't eaten anything today.

"Want to grab a bite in the cafeteria?" Atticus suggested.

"Yes. I suppose I might as well break in the cafeteria here."

Even though she should make an excuse, because she didn't want to get attached to him or this place, she didn't want to be alone. Her first patient in Fort Little Buffalo almost died, and she was still a bit shaken up.

CHAPTER SIX

THE CAFETERIA WAS OPEN, but busy, and they didn't have a place to sit down at the time they made their way down there. So they both grabbed a sandwich, and then Atticus got called away. Penny was a bit disappointed, but as she ate her sandwich in her office, she thought it was for the best.

The last time she got involved with a coworker like this, it ended all wrong. And then she was angry at herself for letting thoughts of Walter and what happened in Calgary flash through her mind again.

The whole affair ended a month ago.

As soon as she found out he was married, she'd ended it, and she tried to go on with her normal life in Calgary. When she returned, she wanted to do it with her head held high, prove to them all she was okay, but she'd have to be careful.

After making a check on Marcus and giving instructions to the night shift to call her if anything changed, she headed straight for her temporary lodging.

It was a nice walk from the hospital. Not far at all.

The temperature was dropping, and the sun was already setting earlier and earlier the closer they got to the autumn equinox. She'd forgotten that the further north they got, the darker it got in the winter months.

She'd definitely picked the wrong time to work up in the Northwest Territories, but on the bright side, she wouldn't have to contend with bugs.

Penny laughed at that as she pulled up the hood on her sweater and shoved her hands in her pockets.

When she got back to her place, she changed into her workout clothes and decided that tonight she would exhaust herself at the recreation center so that she could sleep and not think about Dr. Atticus Spike.

She didn't want to think about the shared smiles, or how in tune they had been with Marcus. Or how attentive he had been during the testing.

It was easy to work with him, compared to others she had worked with in Calgary.

Penny drove her car over to the recreation center because she didn't want to walk home in the dark. Especially when she wasn't overly familiar with Fort Little Buffalo yet.

When she got there, she was set up with a pass so that she could use the small gym they had. In one of the gymnasiums, there was a floor hockey practice happening for young kids.

She smiled as she watched them and saw all the moms off to the sidelines with their coffee cups. She was a bit envious of them and their kids. It just seemed impossible now. Especially when she just didn't want to put her heart at risk or put her child at risk of growing up without the love of one parent. Of being a pariah, the shame of a parent.

Penny was keenly aware of how that felt.

How it hurt.

She choked back the lump in her throat and held back the unshed tears, refusing to cry over a man who wasn't man enough to tell her the truth or a father who thought her worthless. No matter how much it hurt.

Penny put her purse and jacket in a locker and then changed into her sneakers before heading out into the gym. All she wanted to do was run on the treadmill and listen to her music. That would tire her out so she could sleep and would completely clear her mind and center her focus on what she needed to do while she was in town.

And that was work.

She made her way across the gym floor, and out of the corner of her eye, she caught sight of Atticus at the weights, deadlifting. As much as she wanted to look away, she just couldn't tear her gaze from him, of the glistening muscles of his forearms as he squatted down and lifted the bar with the loaded weights.

Her mouth went dry as she watched him, and her pulse began to race.

You need to look away.

Penny listened to that voice in her head and quietly walked over to the treadmill. Thankfully, he was too busy to notice her, and she was able to get on a machine, plug in her music and run.

Of course, instead of hearing the lyrics to her music, all she could think about was him. Why were the fates so determined to throw them together?

It's a small town.

And that was the kicker.

If she met him in a city hospital, she'd be able to avoid him more easily, and she would probably never run into him in a large city like Calgary. She rarely saw her coworkers after their shifts were over.

Fort Little Buffalo wasn't that large.

And there wasn't that much to do.

And his cabin probably only had things like sticks and stones to work out with. She smiled to herself, laughing at that. When she glanced up in the mirror in front of her, he was gone, and she let out a sigh of relief.

She adjusted the speed on the treadmill, and when she looked up, Atticus was standing next to her.

"Holy heck!" she cried out. She shut down her treadmill and pulled out her earbuds. "You scared the living daylights out of me."

Atticus grinned. "Sorry. I came over here to do my cardio and saw you."

"Yeah, well, I didn't really think it was appropriate to sneak up on someone lifting heavy weights."

"You saw that, did you?" There was a twinkle in his eyes.

"Get over yourself," she muttered. "Of course I saw you. You seem to be thinking the same thing I am. You're always around."

"I could say the same thing about you," he responded, climbing up onto the treadmill beside her. "Usually, this time of day, I have the gym to myself while everyone's at the ball hockey."

"Sorry to invade your space." She started her machine again. "Since I didn't get my run this morning, I wanted to get one in tonight."

"I understand."

"I'm surprised to see you here," she quipped. "I thought you'd be out chopping wood for the winter. Tanning hides or smoking meat."

"I do that every other year. I'm good for now, but don't make fun of chopping wood. It helps with accuracy and mental concentration. Plus, it helps strengthen the forearms and wrists." He held out one of his muscular forearms.

"I'm sure," she said, tearing her eyes from him.

"What do you do to keep your dexterity?" he asked.

"I crochet," she stated.

He cocked an eyebrow, jogging beside her. "Seriously?"

"Yes." She grinned. "Maybe I can crochet you a rug for your cabin."

"What kind of cabin do you think I live in?"

he asked. "Do you think I'm some kind of home-steader or something?"

"The first time I saw you, you looked like a woodsman coming out of the forest. I told you this. With that beard and flannel shirt. Plus, you told me you're out of town and your great-grandfather built it."

Atticus chuckled. "Okay, it's a bit rustic, but I assure you I have internet and satellite."

"You live off the grid, don't you?"

"I have solar panels." Atticus continued running beside her, and she tried not to watch him. "I think you need to come and see the cabin for yourself."

As much as there was a part of her that wanted to see the cabin, there was also the part that was hurt and was telling her to run, that she shouldn't be trying to make a friend here. When she left Fort Little Buffalo in six months' time, she didn't want anything holding her back. And they'd agreed to keep it professional. Cordial, but professional.

"We'll see," she replied stiffly, staring ahead at the mirror in front of her.

Something was telling her that Atticus was not like Walter. She wasn't sure if he was married, he didn't wear a ring, but that didn't mean anything.

Walter didn't wear his ring. She'd made an assumption there, and look where it had got her. She wouldn't fall for a man she knew nothing about, no matter how attracted she was to him.

"Atticus?" a female voice called out.

Penny looked up at the mirror to see a beautiful blonde woman come into the gym. She looked like one of the moms she had passed by on her way in.

See. He has someone.

The disappointment was surprising to her, and also the little bubble of jealously that sprang up.

What did you expect? He's handsome and she's pretty.

The blonde woman spotted them and made her way over to the treadmills.

"Atticus, are you ready to go home?" the woman asked.

"I can walk home," Atticus responded.

The woman crossed her arms. "You live five miles outside of town, in the bush. I don't think so."

"I've done it before. Besides, I can always hit up my new coworker here for a ride."

Penny's face flushed with heat. She did not want to be dragged into this lovers' quarrel or whatever it was. She shut off her machine and turned to face the woman. She was not going to be thought of as a man stealer.

It was bad enough everyone at the hospital in Calgary already thought that about her.

"Hi, I'm Dr. Penny Burman. I'm new to Fort Little Buffalo." She might as well introduce herself and make it known that she wasn't a threat to this woman.

The woman smiled and took Penny's outstretched

hand. "Ah, so you're the one Atticus mentioned, the one Horatio has taken a liking to."

"I suppose I am."

"Since my brother is so socially awkward, I'm Ginny Beauchamp, and I'm the one who brings his lazy hide to the gym when my youngest has ball hockey."

His sister?

She would've never guessed that they were brother and sister because they seemed so dissimilar. Ginny exuded a warmth that Atticus did not.

Atticus stopped running and shut off the machine. "Sorry, yes, this is my sister, and yes, she does bring my sorry butt out here when she comes, and I appreciate it."

Ginny narrowed her eyes at her brother. "We're ready to go."

"I can take him home," Penny offered, surprising herself. She didn't know why she'd blurted that out.

Atticus turned to her. "You don't have to. I was only teasing."

"I don't mind." She stepped off the treadmill. "I'm just going to use the shower, and then I'll be ready to go. Ginny, it was a pleasure to meet you."

Ginny smiled at her. It was warm and friendly. "It's great to meet you too, Dr. Burman. I hope that I'll be seeing a lot more of you."

Penny nodded and made her way to the women's locker room to put some distance between herself and Atticus and his sister.

No matter how she tried to escape him, he was always there. She should've let him walk home, but that wasn't safe. She couldn't allow the world's most renowned, reclusive neonatologist to get carried off by a wolf or a moose or something. Or she should've let him go with his sister, but Penny had offered, and she didn't go back on her word.

And that's how she rationalized getting sucked back into spending more time with Atticus. It was the right thing to do, even though she did like being around him. She was just angry at herself because of that.

Atticus was mentally kicking himself for suggesting that Penny drive him home. He'd meant it as a joke to annoy his sister. He really didn't think that Penny would take him up on that. He had felt bad that their lunch today hadn't panned out.

As he ate his subpar sandwich alone in his office, he'd thought it was for the best that he got called away, because he'd forgotten himself for a brief moment when he invited her for lunch. And the reason he forgot himself was that he had just been overcome with admiration for her during Marcus's emergency and the tracheostomy procedure.

Penny had handled herself with calm and put her trust completely in him and the other staff in the room. The whole procedure happened seamlessly. There had been other times when Atticus had worked with new pediatricians or even just ones that were spending a short amount of time here like Penny was, and they hadn't been so easy to work with.

They either didn't know what to do in the situation like this, in a small hospital, when it was all-hands-on-deck, or they knew exactly what to do and didn't want others interfering, so they would bark orders.

Penny was no shrinking violet. That was clear in the way she talked with him. But she had a gentle, kind bedside manner. She was completely empathetic to the patients, their families and the staff.

There were times when his own empathy was so great that it drained him. That it just ate away at him to lose a patient or see a child hurt. He had worked hard to build that thick skin, but sometimes it wasn't enough.

All he could think about was those twins. The conjoined twins who were fused near the spine and shared kidneys. He'd done a separation like that before and he was confident, but then there was always a case of unforeseen complications. Things that surgeons wish they could predict and couldn't.

It pained his soul when he lost a child, but it was something he was never going to give up on. He wanted to save every life that he could and remember each and every child he couldn't save.

Atticus quickly showered in the men's changing room and then went outside. Penny was waiting beside her car. It was a small car that was better suited for city driving and not for the winters that would rip through the north.

At least she had snow tires, but he knew that Calgary was no stranger to snow either.

"If you were staying longer, I would suggest getting a truck over that sedan," he said.

"I figured as much. I don't plan on leaving town once the snow flies."

"That's good, because you won't get very far."

Penny rolled her eyes. "You keep up with the criticisms and I'll make you walk home."

He grinned. He really liked her quick wit. He had missed bantering with someone. Sasha didn't banter.

"Are you hungry? I know a great café where we can grab a bite. It's my treat since you're driving me home. I promise no more criticisms."

"Sure." He climbed into the passenger side. She got in behind the wheel. "Where am I headed?"

"Seymour Street. About two blocks that way. It's the Blackbird Café."

"Oh, yeah, I heard that was good." She turned the ignition and drove over to the Blackbird Café, parking on the street in front of the small restaurant. Again, it didn't look like much from the outside, but he had a feeling she would like the inside.

Everyone did.

It was eclectic and unique, plus the food was amazing. The chef was from this town like him, but Jonah had studied at a culinary school in Montreal and then in Europe. He had returned to his roots to bring fine dining to Fort Little Buffalo.

And the residents were indeed happy for that.

Atticus opened the door for Penny, and as she stepped in, she was surprised.

"Oh, wow, it's stunning in here. It's like a hipster place out of the city."

The decor was eclectic, a mix of old and new. Modern lines, but thrift store furniture. Mismatched chairs and tables with modern tableware.

"Jonah is Dene, and a lot of his food is influenced by his time in Europe and a mix of his Indigenous ancestry."

Penny's eyes sparkled in the dim light. "I can't wait to try it!"

Jonah's wife Lacey helped run it. Lacey grinned brightly when she saw them. "Atticus, you finally decided to actually bring someone here to eat with you!"

Atticus groaned.

Lacey was from Paris. She had met Jonah when he was over there, and the two of them had fallen in love. Lacey moved her whole world to make Jonah's dream come true. As far as Atticus was concerned, there weren't many women like Lacey.

He knew now, Sasha would never have done that for him. Not for Fort Little Buffalo. Sasha's idea of living the dream only dealt with large cities with impressive hospitals. Sasha followed the money.

He'd grown up with Jonah, so naturally he knew

Lacey well, and Lacey, just like his sister Ginny, seemed to revel in matchmaking.

Something he had no interest in. With all his old friends married and happy, he mostly kept to himself.

"This is my colleague, Dr. Penny Burman. She's staying in Fort Little Buffalo for the next six months before she heads back to Calgary," Atticus responded, dodging the little dig about him usually coming to the Blackbird Café alone.

Lacey smiled and took Penny's hand. "A pleasure to meet you, Dr. Burman."

"Penny is fine," Penny said. "Your accent, are you from France?"

Lacey's face lit up. "*Oui*, I was born and raised in Paris. I planned to live there my whole life until I met a gorgeous man from northern Canada who was a brilliant chef. He whisked me off my feet, and I gladly followed him here. I love it here; this is home now. Even if it isn't as exciting as Paris."

"I'm sure," Penny said.

"I'll show you to a nice quiet booth." Lacey turned, and they followed her through the busy café to a booth tucked in the corner. "This is Atticus's usual spot where he mopes."

"I don't mope," Atticus grumbled, but he looked over at Penny, and she was laughing quietly behind her hand. He sighed. "Okay, I don't mope much, then."

They took a seat across from each other, and Lacey handed them the single-page menus.

"We have a set menu here, but there are a couple of choices. We change the menu weekly, depending on what ingredients Jonah can get," Lacey explained.

"It sounds great," Penny responded.

Lacey nodded. "I'll be back soon. Take your time, and Atticus, I'll let Jonah know you're here."

Atticus groaned as she walked away.

"Why are you groaning?" Penny asked.

"Because she's going to let Jonah know that I'm here."

"And?"

"It's a double meaning."

"How is it a double meaning?" she asked.

"Lacey is going tell Jonah that I'm here with a woman. Jonah and Lacey are perpetual matchmakers."

Penny's eyes widened, and she seemed to be a bit horrified by that thought too. "Oh. I see."

He chuckled softly. "So, you're not in favor of matchmaking friends?"

"No," Penny said quickly. "I just got out of a… I'm not interested in being set up. No offense."

"None taken. I feel exactly the same. I was engaged once, and that was close enough for me." And then he realized that he had spilled the beans about Sasha, something he didn't want to do. He didn't like talking about Sasha to anyone.

Not his parents, not Ginny. No one.

And he was angry he'd let it slip out.

"Well, I didn't get engaged," Penny said, with bitterness in her voice. "Though it's kind of hard to get engaged to someone who is already married."

Atticus was surprised. "Married?"

She nodded, red blooming in her cheeks, and he wasn't sure if it was embarrassment or just anger, or maybe it was a mix of both. "It's why I'm here. My hospital wanted to keep Walter, and his wife had loads of money to donate. She wanted me gone, but there were no grounds to terminate me, so they offered me a locum position here in Fort Little Buffalo for six months or…"

"Wow," Atticus stated. "I should be surprised, but I'm not. Hospital politics are not for me."

"Same," she responded dryly.

"Is this ex of yours the one who has been contacting you?" Atticus asked gently.

"Yes."

"What a jerk," he snapped.

"The thing is…my job means so much to me. I want to show my hospital I am a team player."

He was angry that Penny's confidence was shaken.

She shouldn't feel that way. Penny was talented, and he wished she could see that her worth was so much more than what a big-city hospital thought of her. What her colleagues thought of her.

In that way, Penny reminded him of Sasha. He knew then that Penny wouldn't stay here.

"If Calgary can't see that, they're fools," he said. "You don't owe this Walter guy anything."

Penny's expression softened. "Thanks."

Atticus nodded and awkwardly looked down at his menu. His pulse raced as he thought about comforting her. He wanted to.

He wanted to help her see the worth that he saw in her, even just after knowing her for a short time.

"Is that why you disappeared?" she asked. "Because your engagement ended?"

A lump formed in the pit of his stomach, and his whole body went rigid. He really didn't like to talk about it. And he hadn't talked about it in so long.

"Partly." He sighed, dragging a hand through his hair. "When those twins…"

Even now it was hard to form the words. Even though it hadn't been his fault what happened. The autopsy had cleared him.

"If they were anyone else's children then such attention wouldn't have been on you, you mean," Penny said softly. Her voice was full of understanding. Outside of the people at Fort Little Buffalo Hospital and his family, no one was so caring with him.

No one understood it.

"Exactly. People I trusted turned on me. People I thought were family didn't really want to be around me anymore. I had no more influence, no more sway, and because of the publicity…the wrong kind of publicity…and an unsupportive hospital board of directors, my practice was dwindling. I still had patients, but the board felt the damage was done. See, Canadian medical practices and US medical practices vis-à-vis payments are different."

Penny nodded, and then she reached out and took his hand in hers. Just gently squeezing it. It sent a curl of heat through his veins. Her touch was so soft, and it was so reassuring. "It wasn't your fault. I hope you know that."

"I do," he said, and he drew his hand back. He didn't want to, but if he continued to touch her, to let her comfort him, it would be harder to push her away. And he had to keep her at arm's length.

"I'm sorry that happened to you. You were…you *are* a brilliant pediatrician and neonatologist. I remember reading about how that premature baby with the organs born outside had no chance of survival, until you took the case on and the baby made it. When I read that case in my first year of residency, I knew exactly what I wanted to be, what I wanted to do. You were a young surgeon doing groundbreaking research."

A secret thrill coursed through him at her kind words. That case of the baby with the omphalocele, delivered at twenty-seven weeks, had been his first real test as a new neonatologist. Other surgeons had written the baby off, but Atticus had known that baby was a fighter and they were going to make it.

And he'd made sure of it.

He hadn't thought of that case in years, but the nice memory flooded his brain instead of the conjoined twins and the heartache Sasha had caused in him. The memories that haunted him. It was nice that Penny brought that out in him.

Lacey came back, all smiles. "Have you guys decided which of the two options you both want to try?"

Atticus glanced down at the menu. "I'll have the bison."

Lacey nodded and turned to Penny. "What would you like, *cherie*?"

"The wild turkey sounds fantastic! I would like to try that."

"That is one of Jonah's specialties. Would you like any wine? We managed to get some up from Niagara recently."

"What would you recommend?" Atticus asked. "Because I swear every time I pick something you just choose for me anyways."

Penny laughed softly and Lacey grinned, taking back the menus.

"A wise decision, Dr. Spike," Lacey said. "You always choose wrong."

Penny was still laughing as Lacey left.

"I'm disappointed, you know," Penny said.

"In what?" Atticus asked.

"I thought you were some kind of hermit mountain man."

He chuckled. "I would rather be some days, but when you move back home, even to hide, everyone knows your name. For the most part I do try to keep to myself."

Penny looked unconvinced. "I still think it makes a better story if the famous Dr. Atticus Spike disappeared into the north to become a mountain man."

"Don't say that," he said quietly.

"Famous?" she asked gently.

He nodded. "I am proud of my work, and I know what happened wasn't my fault, but fame comes with an awful price. People only see what they want to see. They don't know the real me."

And the truth of the matter was, he wouldn't let people see the real him. For so many years, he thought it was his work. That's what he thought defined him. In school, when he was working toward scholarships and excellent grades to get into university and medical school, his identity was tied into his academic rigor.

For five years, he'd felt lost, and he wasn't even sure who he was anymore or what he felt besides numb.

"We all make mistakes; I fell for a married man, and you trusted the wrong people. Actually, I trusted the wrong people too. I won't let that happen again," she said firmly.

"That I understand."

Trust was hard to come by once it was lost. Penny was unlikely to trust anyone again, and it saddened him, but he did understand that loss. His had been lost for some time.

Penny was pleased with the small café's dinner. She had never had wild turkey before, but it was so tender, and the presentation was something like out of Europe.

The café was extraordinarily busy, so she never got to meet the chef, though he waved once when he came out. She could tell that Atticus was visibly relieved, and she was disappointed that she didn't meet his childhood friend.

She wanted to know what juicy tidbits Jonah might have imparted to her.

You don't need to know that.

And the little voice in her head reminded her that no, she didn't need to know that. She wasn't here to get to know Atticus on a personal level. She didn't need to know about his life growing up here.

The problem was, it was so easy to fall into a conversation with him, and the more they talked, the more she understood why he retreated back home after what happened. It scared her that a big hospital like the one in Boston would side with the money over the surgeon, but then the more she thought about it, the more she realized that's exactly what had happened to her.

The children's hospital wanted Walter and his surgical skills, his research and the money his wife had for their hospital. Penny was no one.

Something she felt keenly.

When her father left, that's exactly what she'd felt like.

No one.

Nothing.

She wasn't important enough to him.

She buried those emotions deep down inside her again, refusing to let them out. She was angry that they seemed to be resurfacing more frequently since Walter's betrayal and her arrival in Fort Little Buffalo.

Atticus paid for the bill, because she was driving him out to his cabin.

When they got outside, the temperature had dropped, and there was a chill to the air. It burned her lungs just inhaling.

Atticus sucked in a deep breath. "Snow is in the air."

"Snow?" Penny asked.

He nodded. "It won't last when it comes, but it's coming. Our Indian summer is over."

"I know winter comes swiftly here compared to Calgary, but I'm still not mentally ready for it."

"Well, I'm glad you have snow tires on."

"Yes. I'm ready for it, just I'm also not…"

He laughed softly. "I understand."

She hurried to her car and got in, turning on the heat. Atticus climbed in the passenger side and then punched in the coordinates of his cabin into her GPS, which she was thankful for. Fort Little

Buffalo and neighboring towns like Fort Smith and Fort Fitzgerald were surrounded by Wood Buffalo, which was one of Canada's largest dark night preserves.

When darkness fell, it was *really* dark.

Penny wasn't quite used to such an all-consuming darkness, and she became all the more aware of that as they drove away from town. She was very glad for high beams as she approached the hidden driveway of Atticus's cabin.

"It's not too far off the road," he said.

"You are completely surrounded by trees."

"Just the way I like it," he said, and even though she couldn't see him in the shadows, she knew he was smiling.

Finally they came to a small clearing, and she could see the outdoor lights that were solar-powered on and reflectors marking the edges of his driveway where his truck was. She quickly made a turn, so she didn't have to back out of the narrow drive, and parked.

"Thanks for the ride," he said. "One day you'll have to come over and see my homestead."

The offer caught her off guard, and she was really tempted to. "I'd like that. One day. Thank you for dinner."

Atticus nodded and then leaned over. She could feel the warmth of his breath on her neck. It sent a tingle of desire through her, and she wanted to pull him close and kiss him on the lips. She leaned in, closing her eyes. Hoping for something, though knowing she shouldn't want it.

"Good night, Penny."

Atticus slipped out of the car, making his way up the drive to his house. The outdoor sensor light came on, and she could make out his shadow disappearing into the house and hear Horatio's happy barking that he'd returned home.

Penny's pulse was hammering in her ears. She felt foolish for thinking he was going to kiss her. She'd forgotten herself and the walls she'd built. How could she be so foolish to think about kissing a man she barely knew? When she couldn't trust that there was no chance of being hurt once again?

This was not keeping her distance from him.

This was not just being friends with him. This was creeping into something more, and she didn't like it. She wasn't going to let this happen again. She wasn't a fool.

She drove away from his cabin.

As she did, an aurora burst across the sky, unfurling like a ribbon of green brilliance, and her mind played a picture for her as she drove away, she thought about how romantic it would be to kiss Atticus under the northern lights.

It was just a fantasy, though.

Things like that rarely happened, at least not for her.

CHAPTER SEVEN

One week later

ATTICUS HAD BEEN RIGHT. It had snowed, but it didn't stick, and instead Fort Little Buffalo had had a strange bout of warm weather. There seemed to be no end in sight. Penny didn't mind the unseasonable heat that the rest of the residents were complaining about.

Ever since Atticus had leaned over and she'd mistakenly thought he was going to kiss her, she had been trying to avoid him, throwing herself into her work. Work and avoiding Walter's messages didn't take her mind off her misstep at all. She really didn't know what she was thinking. She hadn't seen much of Atticus, except maybe passing in the hall, but he would look away when she came by.

So he was obviously uncomfortable too with what had almost unfolded.

Penny was both relieved and upset by that, and she was annoyed that she was disappointed by his response.

What do you expect? And she shook that thought away, because she really didn't know what she expected.

All she wanted from her short time here in Fort

Little Buffalo was to work, and so that's exactly what she did. She worked in the pediatric clinic and saw a few ear infections and diaper rashes, she completed routine vaccinations, and there were a few pediatric migraines which she suspected were due to the fluctuating barometric changes.

After her shift was done, she would walk back to her little home and make herself a simple dinner, take her tea and enjoy the cooler nights.

She had gotten into a nice, albeit boring, routine, and she was okay with that. That had been her plan since she'd agreed to come up here.

Penny finished her charting in her temporary office when there was a knock at the door. She glanced up to see Pam, one of the administrative secretaries, at the door.

"Hey, Pam." Penny stood up and opened her door wider. "What can I help you with?"

"This fax just came in for you from Yellowknife, from an environmental firm that did testing at Marcus's house for mold."

Penny took the report from Pam. "Thanks, Pam."

Pam nodded and left. Penny shut the door and read the report. Her heart sank when she saw that it was *Stachybotrys chartarum* in the air at Marcus's house. The firm that did the testing sent someone down and found it was embedded into the wood. They recommend that the house be torn down and rebuilt.

Black mold was everywhere, and Penny was actually shocked that no one else had gotten sick in the house.

She grabbed Marcus's chart and left her office, making her way to her patient's room. She had removed his tracheostomy tube, and he'd been breathing well on his own for the last two days. She was about to see about discharging him today, but now she had to break it to the family that their home was toxic, and if they took Marcus back there, he would have another reaction.

At least the spores were out of his lungs now after a week of antibiotics and medicine that had cleared his lungs.

Penny knocked on their door, and Marcus's mother, Josephine, called her in.

"Dr. Burman, we were hoping to see you today," Josephine said. "This is my husband, Kenneth."

Penny reached out and took Kenneth's hand. He looked pale, and his skin was clammy.

"You okay, Kenneth?" Penny asked.

"I had a bad nosebleed last night before I took the plane this morning and an awful headache, but I think that's just because of the change in temperature," Kenneth said.

"You get nosebleeds a lot lately?" Penny asked.

Josephine and Kenneth exchanged worried glances. Kenneth nodded. "A lot, since the flood."

Penny sighed and handed them the report. "Your home is full of *Stachybotrys chartarum* or black mold. It's highly toxic. Marcus's issues are from that. After his anaphylactic reaction to mold, I had his lungs x-rayed, and they were cloudy. So we started him on antibiotics, and his lungs are clear, but on testing after his bronchoscopy, we found spores from the mold."

Josephine gasped and stared at the paper. "What do we do?"

"The environmental team that went down and did further testing, they suggest the house comes down and a new one put in its place."

Kenneth sighed. "I had been thinking that. Insurance said they would cover it, but it takes so long to get one built up here."

"I think we can push the matter. Marcus can't go back home. He'll have another reaction, and it'll be even more severe. And Kenneth, I think your headache is from your exposure to it. You were there helping remove drywall, right, showing the team the house?"

Kenneth sighed, "I've been trying to make repairs and seal it so if the river floods, we're more protected."

"Do you have somewhere else to stay?" Penny asked.

Josephine nodded. "My parents in Fort Smith can take us until the house is rebuilt."

Penny nodded. "Good. Take Marcus there and don't let him back in the house. Since you'll be in

Fort Smith, he'll be close by, and I can check in on him."

Josephine smiled. "Thank you, Dr. Burman. We would've still assumed it was asthma, and…"

Penny reached out and hugged Josephine, who had broken down in tears. "It's okay."

Penny then made her way to Marcus's bedside and took his hand. Marcus was smiling at her, but still wasn't talking much since the tracheostomy. She knew his vocal cords were fine and it was just a scared five-year-old, but she gazed down at the sweet dark-haired boy and squeezed his hand back.

"You're going to be okay, Marcus."

Marcus beamed and nodded.

"Thank you, Dr. Burman," Kenneth said, shaking her hand. "For all your help. We're very fortunate you came here."

Penny nodded. "I'll get your discharge papers ready."

She slipped out of the room, glancing back at the family, who in spite of having their world turned upside down, were happy. A pang of jealousy hit her.

Family like that was something she'd always wanted.

Something she'd always dreamed about, but that was just the thing.

It was just a dream.

She wasn't destined for a happily-ever-after, and

she was too scared to reach out and try to get that fairy-tale ending she'd always hoped for.

"Dr. Burman," a nurse called out. "We need you in the pediatric emergency room."

"Coming." Penny set her chart in her office and then followed the nurse quickly through the short hall. In one of the trauma rooms, all the curtains were closed, and she could hear the worried cries of a mother.

She entered the room and saw a tiny baby on the bed. Maybe about a week or so old. The baby was yellow, and its stomach was distended.

"What do we have here?" Penny asked as she pulled on a trauma gown.

"Patient is Sophie Leblanc," the nurse said. "She's twelve days old. She was born at home by a local midwife. Mother noticed the baby was jaundiced, unresponsive with a distended belly. Dark urine and pale stools."

"I have the diaper, her last diaper to show," Sophie's mother said frantically.

Penny glanced over at the diaper and saw the dark urine staining it and the gray stool. Usually newborns were having meconium and dark seedy stools in the first few days of life.

This was abnormal.

There were a million things going on in her head. In her mind, she was flicking through medical cases, reports, things she had seen, and trying to figure out what could cause this in a young infant. The only thing she came back to was biliary atresia, which meant one of the bile ducts was blocked.

The only way she could determine if it was biliary atresia was to run blood work, a liver biopsy, and an ultrasound of the baby.

There were only two options for biliary atresia. The Kasai procedure, which took part of the baby's bowel to form a drain for the blocked duct, or a liver transplant. The Kasai procedure was successful in infants under three months and only if the blocked ducts were extrahepatic, meaning that they were outside the liver. If they were intrahepatic, or inside the liver, children most often needed a liver transplant right away. The Kasai bought the child time, but she would still eventually need a transplant.

Penny had done the Kasai procedure three times.

And she had done a liver transplant on a young infant once.

The trick was finding the suitable liver in time before toxins built up too much, making them deadly.

She did know, having read many operative reports, that Dr. Atticus Spike was one of the best at the Kasai procedure, and he had probably done more liver transplants than she had.

"Page Dr. Spike for me," Penny whispered to one of the nurses.

"Right away, Dr. Burman." The nurse slipped out of the room.

"What's wrong with my baby?" Sophie's frantic mother asked.

"I don't know yet," Penny said gently as she palpated the baby's abdomen. "We're going to run some tests. Okay?"

Sophie's Mom nodded.

Atticus came into the room. He was distracted, and his face was unreadable. Their gazes locked across the trauma pod, and in that instant, she could feel a coil of heat unfurl in her belly. Her skin flushed as she thought of how she had wanted to kiss him in that moment in her car. And how silly she'd felt when he pulled away.

She tore her gaze away from him.

Right now, she had more important things to focus on.

Atticus had been avoiding Penny for a week. Ever since he had made that foolish blunder of almost kissing her. He didn't know what came over him. He'd had such a good time with her at the Blackbird Café. Then he'd thought better about kissing her and and he'd pulled away even though she was leaning in to kiss him too.

Embarrassing her.

Afterwards he just kicked himself internally for being such a fool. Now she was avoiding him too it seemed. Rightfully so. She had trust issues, and he'd acted foolish, and why would someone like Penny be interested in him? Especially when he knew her situation and what had happened to her in Calgary.

It was better if Atticus gave her space. She seemed to be avoiding him too, so he was surprised when she requested his presence in the emergency room. He went, because it was work, but then he saw the tinge of pink in her cheeks, and he was hit with the keen memory of how soft her skin was when they shook hands a week ago.

And he wondered how sweet she would taste if he did kiss her like he wanted to.

"What's the status?"

"Female infant, born twelve days ago. Presenting with jaundice, dark urine and pale stools. Abdomen is rigid and distended. Ocular exam shows the whites of the eyes are yellowing, and the liver appears rigid under palpation," Penny said over her shoulder.

Atticus pulled on a gown and gloves and took a look at the lethargic infant. Intravenous lines had been started, and the baby had an oxygen mask on and was being given medicine, so the wee thing didn't feel any pain and stress.

"You've ordered a blood test with a biliary count?" Atticus asked.

Penny nodded, meeting his gaze. "I think an ultrasound and a liver biopsy are in order."

"Agreed. Get the parent's permission, and I'll

have the baby admitted to the neonatal intensive care unit."

Penny nodded, pulled off her gloves and grabbed the forms she'd need. The baby's mother was outside the door. She had been ushered out as the staff had been putting in the intravenous lines and umbilical lines.

Atticus's heart sank seeing how frantic the mother was, but then he saw how gentle Penny was with her. Though he couldn't hear what was being said, he knew the gist. A liver biopsy was invasive, but he knew Penny was thinking the same thing he was about the infant's diagnosis—biliary atresia.

He'd seen it time and time again in Boston.

This was his first time in five years seeing it up here.

They had the facilities to do the Kasai procedure.

For a liver transplant, they would have to airlift the baby to Edmonton or Calgary. Even then, it was risky. He hoped, if it was what Penny and he were both thinking, that the Kasai procedure would save the baby.

A nurse walked off with Sophie's mother, to take her to a room where she could sign the forms in peace and make phone calls and, most importantly, wait in comfort.

Penny came back in the room. "She's consented to the biopsy and everything else."

Atticus nodded. "I'll clear a spot in the operating room so we can get the biopsy done right away. The sooner we know, the better chances we have."

Penny nodded. "I would like to be part of this."

Atticus was shocked. "Why wouldn't you be? You're the patient's doctor."

"Because I haven't done as many Kasai procedures as you. Though I am very skilled at biopsy."

"I have no doubt, Dr. Burman."

Penny looked relieved. "Okay."

And he hated that she seemed to doubt her abilities.

"I will need assistance with the Kasai," he said. "We have to do a Roux-en-Y connection and create an extrahepatic duct. We also have to remove the gallbladder. You will be involved, and you will do the biopsy."

The orderlies wheeled little Sophie off to the neonatal intensive care unit to prep her for her procedures.

Penny looked stunned. "Thank you for letting me be a part of it."

"Why are you so shocked by that?" Atticus asked. "You're a pediatric surgeon. You're not a resident."

"At a bigger hospital, sometimes complicated procedures like this would go to the higher-ranking surgeons. I was still a fairly new surgeon in Calgary."

And he understood that.

It had happened to him when he was new, but

not as often as it would happen to female surgeons and residents. After he wrote an award-winning paper and completed research that made him famous, then he never had to fight for position again.

He'd forgotten that.

"It's not like that here," he said. "I need you in there with me."

Penny smiled, that pink tinge in her cheeks. The one he liked so much, the slight flush of blood that made him want her all the more. She was everything his ex wasn't, and again he continued to question what he ever saw in Sasha.

The flush in her cheeks deepened, and he was fighting the urge to kiss her, just like he had wanted to do in the car a week ago. Only this time he couldn't lean across in a public place and kiss her cheek.

No matter how much he wanted to do that.

"Radiology will be ready soon," Penny said, tearing her gaze away. "I'd better get to the operating room and scrub in, prep for the biopsy."

Atticus took a step back, as if doing that would somehow quell the desire he felt for Penny. He hated that he felt this way about her. How she got through all his defenses.

He ran his hand through his hair. "I will meet you there soon."

Penny nodded, and he watched her walk away, longing for a different time. When he wasn't so scarred by what had been done to him, when he had still been that confident fly-boy of a surgeon, and when she hadn't had her heart broken.

He would try to remain her friend.

Friendship he could handle.

Losing his heart to someone else, someone who intended to leave, he couldn't handle.

CHAPTER EIGHT

ATTICUS MADE HIS way to the operating room after he checked on Sophie. The baby was stable and sedated. She wouldn't feel any pain and hopefully would never remember this rough start to her life.

He knew the midwife, Janice, who had delivered Baby Sophie. Janice was a competent Fort Little Buffalo midwife, and he had no worries that anything had gone wrong there. Sometimes these things just happened.

Those were the very words the doctor had told his parents when his twin sister Andrea had died.

He was going to make sure Sophie had the best care.

He just hoped that little Sophie didn't need a liver transplant immediately.

That was something he didn't want to do.

The wait could be long, and Sophie might not make it.

With the Kasai procedure, she had a good shot of survival. There were never any guarantees, as he knew all too well with what happened in Boston.

Baby Sophie was being wheeled into the operating room. The ultrasound technician was waiting and chatting with Penny. This would be their first time together in the operating room. He had been there with her when she performed Marcus's tracheostomy, but that was different. That was an emergency situation.

It had gone spectacularly well, but this was their first time in a formal operating room setting together, with the rest of the operating room staff.

Not all surgeons worked well together, and not everyone worked well with his team in the operating room. Not that any other surgeon would have a choice here in Fort Little Buffalo. There was one set of operating room staff members for pediatrics.

So he hoped that Penny got along well with everyone and with him.

So far, what he had seen of Penny in the hospital was a good sign. She seemed to get along with everyone. Each person he'd talked to since Penny had arrived liked her. Atticus had high hopes. He finished scrubbing in and entered into the small operating room.

His scrub nurse, Laurie, helped him on with his gown and gloves.

"We're ready to start," Ted, the ultrasound technician, said.

Atticus nodded. "Dr. Burman is leading this biopsy, but I would like some images of the liver done. In particular the duct work."

Ted nodded. "Got it."

The operating room lights were dropped, and Ted applied the gel to Baby Sophie. Atticus came to stand next to Penny, both of them silent as they watched the ultrasound monitor. The images would be read by the radiologist, Dr. Downie, but Atticus knew what he was looking for and had seen enough.

Ted finished his imaging and wiped away the gel. Laurie cleaned and draped where the small incision would be made so that Penny could guide her hollow needle in to take samples.

"All yours, Dr. Burman," Ted remarked.

"Thank you, Ted." Penny stepped up to the surgical field, and the lights were brought back on. "Scalpel."

Laurie handed the scalpel to Penny. Penny made the tiny incision in Baby Sophie's skin, and then Laurie handed her the needle as Atticus held the clamp so she could visualize the liver. It was delicate work, as Sophie was so small.

Penny inserted the needle and proceeded to get the samples.

Atticus watched her work with precision.

She was not lying when she mentioned that she was skilled at delicate biopsies. It was clearly evident in the way she handled the instruments and the way she moved.

He was impressed.

Their gazes locked for a second.

"Nicely done, Dr. Burman. We need to take several samples."

Penny nodded. "I know."

Each sample she took was placed into a test tube

with solution to preserve it, so it could be flown to Yellowknife, where it would be tested by a pathologist.

After all the samples were collected, they were placed in a cooler by one of Fort Little Buffalo's lab technicians who was going to take a chartered flight up to Yellowknife to drop off the samples.

"Tell Yellowknife it's urgent," Atticus said.

The lab tech nodded and exited the operating room. Penny closed the small incision, and then she and Atticus turned little Sophie on her side to apply pressure to the liver, which would help it stop bleeding.

Baby Sophie would remain sedated on her side for a few hours, and Atticus put in an order for UV treatment for the evening to help break up the bilirubin in her system.

"Now we wait," Atticus remarked as Sophie was wheeled from the room.

"What do you think? You were watching those ultrasound images closely," Penny said.

"The radiologist will have to confirm, but I think a bile duct is constricted or blocked, and I think that little Sophie is suffering from biliary atresia."

Penny nodded. "That was my gut instinct too, but when we have all the lab work and the pathology back, we'll know."

"I just hope the Kasai procedure works," Atticus remarked. "There are times when it doesn't, and the child eventually has to be put on the donor list, but the older the child is, the better the prognosis. Sophie still has a long road ahead of her."

"And that's part of the reason why we do what we do." Penny smiled, her pride evident in her voice.

Atticus glanced over at her. She was smiling so sweetly, and it made his heart skip a beat. "Yes. Exactly."

"I'd better get back to charting." She peeled off her surgical gown, tossed it in the receptacle, and made her way out of the operating room into the scrub room. Atticus followed her.

He wanted to apologize to her about what happened last week.

For embarrassing her and himself.

For pulling away from a kiss he so wanted, even if it was for the best.

"You're off tomorrow," he remarked, which was his awkward way of trying to invite her somewhere so he could apologize to her in private.

Still, he was never really good at this kind of thing.

Penny cocked an eyebrow. "I am."

"How about a trip to Pine Lake? See the sinkholes."

She opened her mouth as if to answer, and then her mouth snapped shut. "Do you think that's wise?"

A knot formed in his stomach. "Because of what happened last week?"

Penny leaned against the sink, her arms crossed. "Right. I'm not here for long, and I just got out of… what I thought was going to be a long-term relationship."

"I'm not looking for a relationship. Just friendship," he stated. "Besides, I usually take Horatio there for a swim, and he's been itching to go. The weather has turned nice again. What do you say?"

Say no. Say no.

Except she really didn't know what she was going to do during her time off tomorrow. And truth be told, she had missed working with Atticus this past week when they had been busy and she was purposefully trying to avoid him.

She hadn't had much time to make other friends in Fort Little Buffalo.

It was a lonely existence.

Other than phone calls home to her mother and her half sister, she was alone and isolated up here. It wouldn't hurt to spend some time with him. She had made it clear that she wasn't looking for a relationship, and neither was he.

Friends could go on outings together.

"Okay," she finally said. "What time?"

"One? I can show you around a bit, and you can see the sinkholes before the winter makes the roads a little bit harder to traverse until they freeze."

"There's an ice road?" she asked.

"Fort Fitz to Fort McMurray. It saves a lot of time, but the ice roads can be tricky."

"I have no desire to go on an ice road." She shuddered as she waved her hands under the automatic faucet and began to scrub. "I look forward to the trip and seeing Horatio."

"Good. He'll be pleased to see you too." Atticus began to scrub as she was finishing.

"When do you think we'll hear about the biopsy?" she asked.

"Hopefully in a couple of days," Atticus said. "Yellowknife is pretty good when it comes to rush pediatric biopsies."

Penny nodded. "I'll see you tomorrow."

She left the operating room. Even though it was just a friendly date with a very active dog, her stomach was still full of butterflies. It was a mixture of anticipation and anxiety. She should've told him no, but there was no harm in finding a friend.

Even a friend you were highly attracted to.

Penny didn't see Atticus again that day. She was called to the emergency room a couple of times, but it was nothing as serious as little Sophie. The rest of the day was quiet, and she was thankful for that. It gave her a chance to catch up on paperwork.

It was then she noticed the emails she had left unread.

And they were from Calgary.

From Walter in particular. He'd stopped texting her, but he had continued to email her. She had gotten better at deleting his them since her talk with Atticus in Hay River, but they were still coming.

She had deleted them, and it put her in a foul mood for the rest of her shift. She had no idea why he was reaching out and emailing her. She had already answered all his questions, and she didn't really care what he wanted now. Still, didn't he get the hint? She wasn't going to give him anything. Before, she would've jumped at the chance to help him, before she knew he was a married man and when she fancied herself falling in love with him.

Before he broke her heart.

She had tossed and turned all night over that, and there were a few times in the morning she thought about calling Atticus and canceling her plans with him, but it was too nice a day. The warm weather came back in a freak shift of the southern jet stream. It might be one of the last good, warm days left before the snow and the darkness of winter enveloped them.

She deserved to go out and enjoy herself.

So she tried to forget about Walter and how he had hurt her. She tried to forget about how he was invading her time alone up here and using her, just like he always did, and enjoy her day off playing tourist.

She was waiting outside when Atticus pulled up

in his truck. Horatio was in the back seat, belted in, but he could still stick his head out the window if he stood, which he was. His tail was wagging like crazy and whacking Atticus in the side of his face. Horatio took up the entire back seat.

Horatio let out a howl, almost as if to say *come on*.

"You'd better get in. He knows where we're going, and now he's about thousand times more excited since we're picking you up," Atticus called through the open passenger window, trying to avoid being smacked by a furry tail.

All those bad, anxious feelings that she was feeling about Walter and this jaunt melted away the moment she climbed into the passenger side of Atticus's truck and was met with a huge lick from a big pink tongue and a head over her shoulder, begging to be petted.

"Good to see you too, Horatio," Penny said, patting him.

"Horatio, dude, you need to relax. She's coming with us," Atticus teased.

Horatio responded with a serious side-eye glance and then turned around to sit on his blanket in the back seat as Atticus drove out of town.

"How far is this mysterious sinkhole?" Penny asked.

"About sixty kilometers. So about an hour drive, give or take."

"An hour?" Penny asked. "I thought you said it was local."

"Up here, an hour is local."

"I'm beginning to understand that," Penny mumbled.

"You get to see Fort Smith."

"Is it bigger than Fort Little Buffalo?"

"About the same, and honestly, pretty similar."

"It's interesting that the territorial government decided to put a children's emergency room in Fort Little Buffalo."

Atticus nodded. "Partly my doing when I arrived."

Penny was shocked. "What do you mean, partly your doing?"

"I saw a gap in the area. It's such a long drive to Hay River and an even longer one around Great Slave Lake to Yellowknife. There are many remote villages that surround Wood Buffalo. I was trying to make it more centralized and easier for people to fly in somewhere closer. Take, for example, Marcus's family. What could've happened to him had they waited for the locum pediatrician to pass through? Or what if he had an anaphylactic reaction and they had to fly him into Yellowknife? He might've died. As much as I hate using my name to gain favors, I did just that to turn a little wayside hospital in Fort Little Buffalo into a real functioning pediatric emergency clinic."

She was completely impressed. She'd had no idea, but it had been in the back of her mind since she got here why there was such a place in the southern part of the territory. It just seemed like such an unlikely location, but she understood it now.

And she respected it. Walter wouldn't have cared as passionately about a small community like this.

"In fact, in a couple days, we're being sent up to one of the remote villages. The village doctor and midwife requested pediatricians to attend, and Fort Little Buffalo tries to rotate who goes when. And since I'm the pilot..."

"I'm glad to go and help any way that I can," Penny said quickly. "That's why I'm here. To work."

"I know," he replied quietly.

She had a pang of guilt for putting such an emphasis on *to work*. She had told him that, she'd told herself that, but she didn't know why she was repeating herself. It didn't need repeating, and it made her sad to think of closing herself off to him.

"So, routine vaccinations and checkups, then?" Penny asked.

Atticus nodded. "And some more advanced diagnostics that the town general practitioner would like a second opinion on. Same with the midwife."

That piqued her interest. "I'll look forward to the chance to fly into one of the villages."

"Even if I'm flying?" he asked, winking at her.

"You're a very competent flyer," she said.

He nodded, but as he did, his truck gave a great shudder and started to pull.

"What in the world?" he muttered as he found

a large lay-by in order to bring the truck to a stop. Horatio leaped up and barked.

"What's wrong?" Penny asked.

"I don't know." Atticus turned the ignition, but there was nothing. "Hold on. I carry a scanner."

"You carry a scanner?" Penny asked.

"Well, there's not many auto mechanics out here." He opened the door and jumped out, heading to the bed of his pickup truck, where there was a locked box in the bed. He opened it and pulled out a little machine with wires.

He climbed back in and plugged it in to the dash.

"Besides, a good physician always has diagnostic tools," he grunted.

She laughed nervously, waiting for the code to come up. She wasn't unfamiliar with truck repairs. Her grandpa had taught her how to rebuild an engine. Penny always wondered if he was secretly disappointed that she didn't take that up. Of course, he liked to brag that now she fixed kids rather than engines.

"Dammit," Atticus murmured as he read the code.

"What is it?"

"The alternator. I can do most repairs and carry all the parts for emergencies, but I can't fix an alternator. I've never done it."

"No?" she asked, shocked.

He looked at her with chagrin. "Are you saying that you can?"

"I can and I have. You said you had the parts and tools?"

Atticus's eyes widened. "Yes."

"Well, then I'm going to show you how, Dr. Spike." Penny glanced back at Horatio, who was wagging his tail patiently, his head resting between his paws and his two different-colored eyes so meaningful and full of love. "See, Horatio believes in me."

Atticus glanced at his dog, who raised his head, and then he scrubbed his hand over his face. "Okay, Dr. Burman, if you think you can."

She opened the door. "I don't think. I know."

She stepped outside and climbed up into the bed of the truck to see what Atticus actually had, and she was pleasantly surprised to find everything she needed. Even the new alternator.

"It's like a mechanic shop back here," she announced.

"I carry a lot with me. Just in case, but I haven't had to do an alternator yet."

"As I said, I'm going to show you." Penny reached down into the toolbox and pulled out the tools she needed. "Excellent!"

"What?" Atticus asked, climbing in the bed behind her.

She knelt down and pulled out the tool she was excited about. "You have a cross force wrench. This is a good wrench!"

Horatio stuck his head out the open back window and licked her face, barking because he was excited too. Atticus laughed and shoved his furry head back through the opening.

"You sound like a kid on Christmas Day," he remarked. "All over a wrench."

Penny held up the wrench. "You don't understand. This is going to make taking the belt off the tensioner pulley easier."

Atticus's eyes widened. "Whatever you say, Boss."

"Too right!" She grinned and stood up. "Now, let's get this fixed."

"First, gloves." Atticus ripped open a package of new work gloves. "It'll get dirty and greasy, plus a good surgeon needs to protect their hands."

He tossed her the gloves, which she caught with her free hand. She set down the wrench she was so excited about finding and put on the heavy gloves. Then she grabbed her wrench and the other equipment she'd need to replace this alternator.

She could almost hear her grandfather's voice in her ear.

Atticus leaped over the side and got the hood of the truck popped open. "Disconnect the battery?"

Penny nodded. "Unless you want a real nasty electric shock."

"No thanks," Atticus murmured. He hung a torch light on the hood so they could see the engine better. He proceeded, under her watchful eye, to disconnect the battery. "Done."

"Okay, my turn. We're going to disconnect the wires at the back of the alternator." She reached in and disconnected the wires easily. There was a brief moment when she was worried she might forget how to do this, but then it all came flooding back to her.

The memories of her standing over an engine with her grandfather in his heated shop…

"Penny, you're going to need to know this one day," her grandpa had said.

"Really?" she'd asked in disbelief.

"Yes," he'd said firmly. *"What happens if you get stuck in the middle of nowhere and there is no mechanic? You can do this yourself. It will also save you money to know this. So pay attention and do what I say."*

"Okay."

He'd put his arm around her, smiling down at her.

"You are capable and brilliant, Penny. Never forget it."

Only there were times when she did forget it.

There were times she forgot her own self-worth, because it never ever mattered to her father.

After the dead alternator was disconnected, she pulled up her wrench. "Now comes a tricky part. This wrench will help to remove the belt from the tensioner pulley. It's extremely difficult and requires some torque."

"You strong enough, Dr. Burman?" he asked, a twinkle in his eyes.

"Heck yeah. Just need a box or something to stand on." She glanced around, but Atticus disappeared and returned with an empty milk crate.

"This should work."

"Perfect." She climbed up on top and leaned over. "See, this is the tensioner pulley, and we have to remove this belt to get out the old alternator."

It was stiff. It was hard, just like she remembered, and she was struggling to get the right angle.

"Let me help." Atticus slipped his gloved hands over hers, and a zing of electricity flowed through her. His body pressed tight against him as she teetered on the milk crate over the engine of his truck. Her whole body seemed to come alive, and her heart was racing a mile a minute.

The belt loosed, and they were able to remove it.

"Now the alternator," Penny said, trying to distance herself from him. Atticus stepped back, and she pulled out the old alternator. Handing it to him, she said, "There, one naughty alternator out."

"Now the new one?"

"Yep, we basically work backwards."

Penny reattached the belt and connected the wires to the back of the alternator. Once that was secure, they connected it to the battery.

"Now the test," she said, wiping her brow on the back of her wrist.

"We'll see if you're as good a mechanic as you

are a surgeon," he teased, climbing into the driver's seat.

Penny stepped back as he turned the ignition.

The engine came back to life. Purring beautifully, with no shudder. The new alternator wasn't draining the battery. She did a little mental fist pump.

Atticus turned off the ignition. "Impressive!"

"You owe me dinner. That's my fee."

"Done," he said. "Let's say we get out of here?"

Horatio barked in the back, and she laughed. "Good idea."

They cleaned up their mess and locked it all away. She climbed in, and Horatio greeted her the same way as before. She stroked his head.

"I'm seriously impressed," Atticus said again as they got back on the road to Pine Lake.

"Thank you. My grandfather was always so disappointed I didn't become a mechanic. He said I had the knack."

"You're a mechanic of people…or kids. You repair them."

The comment caught her off guard, because that's what her grandfather had always said about her. A lump formed in her throat, and she brushed away the tears, relieved that Atticus didn't notice. It was a reminder that her grandfather was still there, even though he was gone.

Atticus thought similar to him.

It surprised her.

It pleased her, and she could feel her heart melting. She should be worried, only she wasn't. In this moment, she wanted to savor this heavenly visit that seemed to approve of Atticus, even though she couldn't have him.

CHAPTER NINE

"I THINK I'M in shock," Atticus stated as he turned down the smaller gravel road toward Pine Lake.

Penny chuckled. "You've got to have a variety of skills to be a well-rounded person."

He cocked his head to the side. "True."

A lot of surgeons he'd known wouldn't get their hands dirty outside of the operating room.

He'd meant what he said when he told her that he was impressed by her. The more he got to know her, the more he liked about her. It was no longer just an attraction to a gorgeous woman, though that was still there. It was something more.

He liked her as a person.

It just reaffirmed all his first thoughts about her.

When he had been helping her fix the alternator, he'd felt the heat of her body against him. Smelled the lilac scent of her shampoo, heard her breathing. He'd been so close to her, it had taken all of his strength not to reach out and kiss her, and thinking about her like that was not keeping it professional.

He wasn't quite sure why Penny was affecting him so, and he still didn't like it.

Liar.

He ignored that little voice in his head. The one

that was challenging all the careful walls that he had put in place to protect his heart.

He was happy here in Fort Little Buffalo and happy with the way his life was turning out.

Are you?

"I love autumn in the forest." She sighed.

He glanced over at her. Penny was gazing out the passenger window, and Horatio's head rested on her shoulder over the back seat.

"It is beautiful," he murmured, but he wasn't talking about the leaves of yellow and orange.

It was her.

All her.

He parked and got out of the car, opening the back to undo Horatio's seat belt. Horatio bounded out the back and waited for his leash to go on.

Atticus always made sure to leash him just in case there was a buffalo wandering down on the beach, or a bear.

That was the last thing they needed.

"What a beautiful spot," Penny exclaimed.

"Yeah, it's pretty hidden, but popular with those who know it's here and when the heat gets to be too much. Which is not often."

Horatio led the way down the narrow forested path, out into a little park that overlooked the sinkholes that formed Pine Lake.

Penny stumbled, but he reached back with his free hand and steadied her. Her hands were soft as they curled around his forearms.

"Thanks," she said quietly.

"No problem. The path is uneven."

Horatio was pulling on the leash. Penny let go of his arm, and they continued down the path. Once they broke through the brush, there was beautiful white sand beach. There was no breeze, making the water absolutely still. The blue sky and the bright sun made a perfect reflection of autumn trees and evergreens in the crystal-clear water.

It was quiet and calm.

It was one of his favorite places.

"Oh, wow," Penny whispered as she walked out onto the beach. "I've never seen a place like this before."

He smiled. "It's something, isn't it?"

Penny walked down to the water, and Atticus followed, only because Horatio was pulling him to follow after Penny. Horatio planted himself down on the sand next to Penny, staring up at her with longing.

"What's that over there?" Penny asked.

"The cabin?"

She nodded. "Who owns that slice of heaven?"

"Alberta Parks," he teased. "It's a cabin you can rent. It's a pretty basic one, but that really doesn't matter with that view and the white sand beaches."

"No. That is an ideal place to just think," she said wistfully. "A place to escape."

Atticus bent down and let Horatio off his leash. Horatio ran straight into the water, splashing around and having fun. Atticus tossed a ball, and Horatio swam out after it.

"Do you want to escape?" Atticus asked.

"I did," she sighed sadly.

"What do you mean you did?" he asked, sitting next to her.

"Well, I thought by coming here I could put some distance between Walter and me, but he's been emailing and texting me, as you know." She shook her head, her lips pressed together in a thin line.

"Have you stopped responding to him?" he asked.

"Yes."

"You need to block his number."

"I know." She tucked a loose strand of hair behind her ear. "It's hard to block calls from Calgary, though."

"What do you think he wants?" Atticus asked, annoyed Penny's ex was keeping her tied to the end of a string.

"I don't know what he wants. He made it clear it's not me, though. He wants his wife. Just like my father did."

"And do you really want him that way?" Atticus asked.

Penny cocked an eyebrow. "What do you mean?"

"Did you want him to leave his wife? Did you want him to choose you?"

"I thought I did, for a fraction of a second, but no, you're right. I didn't want him to choose me. I would've never felt right about it. I was angry at him for not telling me he was married. I was an idiot."

"No. You weren't. Trusting, but not an idiot." Atticus sat down next to her in the sand. "In my experience, you can't trust people."

"Some you can," she whispered, but she sounded unsure.

Atticus shook his head. "Maybe family, but... people can be awful."

"And you're escaping people too," she said quietly.

"I'm hardly hiding. I came home."

"Calgary is my home... I guess I could've escaped to my grandparents' property in the foothills near Black Diamond, but I didn't even think of that. My mother lives there now with my grandmother, and I didn't want to go there and have them find out why I was leaving Calgary."

Atticus was surprised. "They don't know?"

She shook her head. Tears welled in her eyes, but she quickly brushed them away. "They don't need to know what a fool I made of myself. And honestly, I don't want my mother to feel heartache. It would break her heart all over again."

Atticus scooted closer to her and put his arm around her instinctively, pulling her close to comfort her. He thought that Penny might pull away, but she didn't. Instead, she rested her head against his shoulder.

And she just stayed here, her head against his shoulder, his arm around her, and they stared out over the lake. His pulse was thundering in his ears, and he wanted to pull her even closer. To protect her. To never let her go. He wanted to apologize for the almost kiss, but it was probably best to forget about it so things didn't get awkward.

They'd both made mistakes that night.

Horatio barked and came bounding up the beach with the ball, soaking wet and heading straight for him.

"Oh, God," Atticus groaned.

Penny began to laugh. "I'm out of here."

She leaped up and took off down the beach, kicking off her flats and running barefoot, laughing as Horatio charged after her, all wet and sandy and smelly. Atticus laughed, watching her run away from his big unruly dog.

Her hair came undone from her braid, blowing out over her shoulders as she laughed and screeched at Horatio, who was in his glory thinking that he had found someone to play with. Penny dodged him and managed to grab the ball, tossing it far into the lake.

Horatio took off after it, and Penny walked back. Atticus stood up and got her shoes for her, knocking the sand out of them. She made her way down to the water to rinse off her feet.

"Here," he said, getting on one knee. "Give me your feet."

She shook the water off, teetered, and then held onto his shoulder to balance as he slipped on her shoes.

"I feel like Cinderella." She giggled.

"You're just as sparkling as her." He stood up and looked down at her. Her cheeks were rosy from running and laughing.

His pulse was roaring, his blood sending fire through his veins, and he looked down into her beautiful dark eyes. He brushed his fingers gently across her cheeks, her skin breaking out in gooseflesh, and she closed her eyes, long dark eyelashes brushing against her cheeks. He bent down and captured her lips with his. She stood on her tiptoes, wrapping her arms around him, leaning into the kiss.

He was lost in the sweet taste of her lips. They were featherlight kisses at first, but deepened into something more. Her arms wrapped around him as he tried to get closer to her.

To connect with her like his body was demanding that he do.

Only, he couldn't give her what she deserved because he couldn't allow his heart to be hurt again. His heart was too scarred, and she'd made it clear that she wasn't going to stay. Calgary and her career were what drove her. Sasha hadn't wanted to be here in Fort Little Buffalo, and someone like Penny wouldn't either. She was still getting over heartbreak too. So many obstacles. Too much pain if he took a risk on her.

Penny stepped away, breaking the kiss, resting her hands on his chest. Her long hair blew and tickled his face.

"I'm sorry," he whispered, trying to regain control over the rush of emotion he felt when he'd finally given in to the desires that he had been fighting. "I don't know what came over me."

"It's okay," she said in a whisper. "I kind of got swept up too, but…"

He was supposed to be apologizing to her about their awkward moment before, not kissing her.

He took a step back. "It can't happen again."

She nodded, her lips still rosy from his kisses. "I want to be friends."

"So do I." Which was true. If he couldn't have her, then he wanted to be her friend, just like they'd agreed before. When he was around her, he didn't feel so lonely, and he looked forward to working with her.

"Good," she said, reaching to tie back her flyaway hair.

His phone began to buzz with an incoming message. He pulled it out of his pocket and opened the message from the hospital.

"What is it?" she asked.

"You got the message too, that the pathology report is in on Sophie."

"And?" Penny asked, crossing her arms.

"Biliary atresia. Thank goodness it's not cancer or something more sinister." He slid his phone back in his pocket. "Radiology said it's the ducts from the gall bladder causing the constriction. A Kasai procedure is very probable."

"And it all depends on how Sophie grows and whether she'll eventually need a liver transplant further down the line. The Kasai at least buys her time." Penny sighed. "It's rough news."

"It does. Now we have to prep for the surgery, but it'll have to wait until after we get back from our flight into the remote village. I can't put that off."

"Understandable."

Horatio came dashing out of the water with his tennis ball in his mouth.

The wind was beginning to pick up, and there was a chill to the air, which made Penny shiver.

"I believe I owe you dinner," Atticus said.

"You do, but I think I want to get back home. Can I take a rain check?" she asked, not meeting his eye.

"Of course. I'll take you back home."

He knew that it had to do with their kiss, and maybe some distance would be good. There would be time for other dinners before she left the north.

* * *

For two days, Penny could not stop thinking about the kiss and the way she had melted in Atticus's arms. She really should've put a stop it. The problem was, when he'd slipped on her shoe, his hand brushing her ankle, and when he'd looked at her the way he did, she was lost.

She'd wanted that kiss just as much as he had.

She was the one who had wrapped her arms around him, encouraging him. She was the one who'd deepened that kiss as anticipation coursed through her veins. Her body seemed to wake up, and she couldn't help herself.

Penny knew that Atticus was blaming himself for taking it too far, but she'd also been a very active participant.

She was angry at herself for falling for Mr. Wrong again.

How do you know he's Mr. Wrong? that annoying little voice in her head was asking her.

That little voice was going to get her into trouble. Where was it when she was with Walter? It was nowhere. It was silent.

Atticus knocked on the door to her office.

"Hey, can I come in?" he asked.

"Sure." Penny's heart began to race.

He came in and shut the door but didn't sit down. "We didn't get to chat much after the lake."

"It's okay. Just friends, right?"

He nodded. "Right."

"Good." She folded her hands to stop them from shaking.

"Would you like to come to my cabin tonight? We can talk. I can make you dinner...to apologize."

"Dinner?" she asked, shocked.

"We can also talk about our trip to Meridian Inlet. Strategize, and I can let you know what to expect when we get there."

She breathed a sigh of relief. "That sounds great."

"So, seven? You remember where I live?"

She nodded. "I do."

"Good." He opened the door. "I'll see you then."

When he left, she let out the breath she was holding. Dinner between friends would go great, and it was a dinner to discuss work. Nothing more.

She could handle this.

Penny threw herself back into her work and prepped for her flight with Atticus up to the remote village on the northeastern arm of Great Slave Lake. Way past Lutselk'e, Meridian Inlet was a robust remote village that had a midwife and a physician, but required fly-in services for the children. At certain times of the year, the general practitioner needed help with wellness checkups and vaccinations.

Other than the long flight alone with Atticus and this awkwardness that had settled between them, she was looking forward to going and help-ing. Hopefully, on the flight, they could talk about Sophie's upcoming surgery.

Penny wanted to be his friend, but she couldn't let this friendship develop into something more. No matter how much a part of her wanted it, it wasn't a good idea. For either of them.

Both she and Atticus had been clear with each other that they had to keep things professional. Her time here was limited.

Does it have to be?

Penny sighed and shook her head. Calgary was her home.

She had plans.

Aspirations.

She was going to show Calgary that they sent her away erroneously. She'd worked hard in Calgary, and she wasn't going to throw it all away.

Calgary was her future.

Not Fort Little Buffalo.

Surprisingly she navigated her way in the dark to Atticus's cabin on the outskirts of town.

A bright full harvest moon helped guide the way. She pulled up to the house and could see Horatio in his fenced dog run, bouncing up and down in the light from the windows.

She laughed and parked her car, pulling out a pie and a bottle of wine.

Atticus came out of the house to meet her.

"Hey, so there's a snafu," he said.

"Oh?"

"My youngest niece, Pamela, is here for the night. Ginny had to take Andrea and Sandy to Hay River for some college night thing. I don't quite know what it entails, and Ginny's husband works in Fort McMurray, so…"

"It's up to you to watch Pamela."

Atticus nodded. "I hope you don't mind, or we can reschedule?"

"I don't mind." Penny smiled. "I happen to like children."

Atticus laughed. "I hope so, given you are a pediatrician."

"I did bring a blackberry pie. I hope she'll like it." She handed it to Atticus.

"She will, but we are having spider wieners in the backyard for dinner."

Penny cocked an eyebrow. "Spider…what?"

"I have chicken hot dogs for you."

"Are yours made of arachnids, then?" she asked, slightly horrified.

Atticus grinned. "No, it's the way it's cooked. Pamela's request. I promise, no spiders."

"It sounds great."

"Come on in." Atticus opened the door and she stepped into his cabin.

It was not what she'd expected. The walls were

log, but there was an open concept living room and kitchen. The kitchen was modern with a gorgeous breakfast bar. There was a large couch and a wood stove crackling with a pleasing fire.

On the large couch sat a little girl who looked to be about nine, wearing a tiara. She popped up over the back of the couch and grinned.

"Hello, are you Uncle Cuss's friend?"

Penny stifled a laugh and looked at Atticus. "Uncle Cuss?"

"Yeah, because he cusses all the time when he's chopping wood or when Horatio runs amok," Pamela said.

Penny was trying not to laugh, while Atticus was rubbing his temples.

"Well, then yes, I'm Uncle Cuss's friend, Penny."

Pamela nodded. "Nice to meet you."

"Penny brought pie for dessert," Atticus said.

Pamela's dark brown eyes lit up. "Yum!"

"I hope you like blackberry?" Penny asked.

Pamela nodded and then turned back to her book.

Penny set the wine down on the counter in the kitchen. "Can I help you with anything?"

"Sure, I can show the secret of spider wieners if you're interested. It's a delicate operation," he teased.

"You can trust me." Penny washed her hands.

There was a twinkle in Atticus's eye and he set

a hot dog down on the cutting board. "Pay attention. Closely."

"I am," Penny acknowledged.

Pamela wandered over and sat down on a stool across from them. "Uncle Cuss, are you sure you know how to do this?"

"Of course," Atticus said. "Why are you so worried?"

"Grandpa does it in a certain way," Pamela answered.

"And who do you think I learned it from? He may be your grandpa, but he's my dad," Atticus teased.

Pamela wrinkled her nose and didn't look convinced.

"He's going to show me," Penny said. "Maybe you could oversee?"

Pamela smiled and nodded. "Sounds good."

"Okay. Now I feel pressure," Atticus teased.

Penny shared a smile with Pamela.

"Fine," Atticus groused. "So you're going to take a hot dog and find the middle."

Penny copied him. "Like this, Dr. Uncle Cuss?"

Pamela giggled behind her hand.

"Exactly. Now slice the lower half, making slits so they're not separated from the top."

"Right."

Atticus leaned over, and she could feel his breath on her neck. It made her blood heat realizing how close he was. How intimate this moment was.

"Good job. What do you think, Pamela?" Atticus asked.

"She's doing good," Pamela agreed. "We have to get the fire on."

"You two do that. I think I got this handled." Penny continued to make the spider wieners.

"Okay." Atticus washed his hands and then scooped his niece up. Pamela placed her tiara on his head.

"Now you're ready, Uncle Cuss," Pamela stated.

"Oh, good." Atticus carried Pamela out through the back door.

Penny peered through the window and saw Atticus with that ridiculous tiara and interacting with his sweet little niece.

It made her heart melt.

Her half sister Priyah had shown her pictures of Raj's kids. She had a niece and a nephew. Both were younger than Pamela.

It made her heart ache not knowing them. They didn't even know she existed.

Atticus had this great family. One that loved and supported him.

She was envious of that, of what she would never have, because the thought of losing her dream of happiness was too scary.

She was finally getting her heart healed.

She knew what to focus on. Her career and getting back to Calgary.

* * *

This was not what he planned when he'd invited Penny over for dinner.

He had a salmon in the fridge. He had a nice wine, and Penny brought some too. He'd made a fire, and then Ginny had called.

He couldn't say no.

At least Penny seemed to have no problems with Pamela's presence.

Sasha hadn't really seemed to like kids, even though she was a pediatric neurosurgeon.

As they roasted hot dogs over the fire to create the spider effect of the wiener curling up, Penny sat close to Pamela so Pamela could show her how to roast the wieners to perfection.

Penny was so sweet with Pamela.

It was nice to have company tonight.

Horatio was curled up at Penny's feet, looking up at them hopefully in case they dropped a hot dog.

This moment was cozy, but with Pamela here, it totally defeated the purpose of talking about work.

Did you really want to talk about work?

He ignored that thought.

"Uh, Atticus?" Penny whispered.

"Hmm?"

Penny nodded at Pamela, slouched over. "She's asleep."

And indeed, Pamela was. Atticus scooped up his niece and carried her into the cabin. He tucked her into his spare bedroom, slipping the tiara off his head. He made his way back outside.

Penny was warming her hands by the fire. Embers were floating up into the darkness. It was a magical, peaceful vision.

"You took off the tiara," Penny teased.

Atticus grinned and ran his hands through his hair. "Yeah, well, it only suits Uncle Cuss for so long."

"You're very sweet with her," Penny said.

"I love them."

"I'm envious. I would like to know my niece and nephew."

"Your brother should blame his father."

Penny smiled weakly. "I suppose. But I do understand about being duped."

"You've got to stop blaming yourself for that. It wasn't your fault. Your ex was the scum for lying to you."

"Thanks." Penny sighed. "Well, tomorrow is a long day. Thank you for the spider wieners. I had no idea they curled like that."

Atticus stood. "Sorry we didn't get to talk about work."

"We can talk on the plane."

Atticus walked Penny to her car. He wanted to kiss her good-night.

He wanted to take her in his arms again, but this wasn't a date, and they'd both agreed to be friends.

So he stepped back from her.

"I'll see you at the airport tomorrow," Atticus said.

"Bright and early." She got in her car and drove away.

Atticus sighed, watching her leave. Heading back into the cabin, he felt a bit lonely.

A bit empty.

Like he always did, but he felt it more keenly now.

CHAPTER TEN

PENNY HAD HAD a great time at Atticus's. His niece Pamela was adorable, and she couldn't remember the last time she'd had such an amazing night.

Probably when her grandpa had been alive.

She parked her car, hefted her knapsack on her back, and made her way to where Atticus's plane was.

He was waiting for her.

He smiled, and her heart skipped a beat. She was hoping they could talk about what happened between them at dinner, but then his niece had been there.

There hadn't been a chance to talk about it.

"Good morning," he said.

"Good morning, Uncle Cuss," she teased.

He groaned. "Thanks for that."

"Did Pamela have a good night?"

"She did. She liked you. Told her mom all about it this morning."

"She's very cute."

"You got everything you need?"

"Emergency supplies like you instructed in your memo. Just on the off chance we'll be caught in bad weather." She glanced up at the sky. "It's been so warm, though…"

"Remember when we had that chilly snap? It can happen that fast, especially further north, but you're right. Probably nothing will happen. It's just good to be prepared."

"Like having an alternator?" she teased.

He winked. "Exactly."

Atticus took her knapsack and secured it in the hold with the other supplies.

There was still a light mist clinging to the ground. The sun was still rising and hadn't burned away the last remnants of the dew. It was like smoke creeping across the ground.

"Ready to go?" he asked.

She nodded. "Yep. I'm looking forward to it."

They climbed into his Murphy Rebel. He handed her the headphones, and she settled in the seat next to him. She focused on the trees outside and thought about what the day would bring in Meridian Inlet.

She was looking forward to seeing more of the territory, especially before the winter snows hit, making travel difficult. It would still be winter when her time was up, and she wasn't looking forward to the drive home, although her mother had promised to fly up and make the journey back south with her.

So she wouldn't be alone.

Being alone had never really bothered her before, but it was more and more lately. Especially after such an enjoyable night with Atticus and Pamela.

Penny was coming to the realization that it wasn't because she had a broken heart. In fact, she hadn't thought much about Walter at all for the last week.

The only things she mourned about her broken heart were that it was an embarrassment and she should've known better. Atticus was right. It wasn't her fault. Walter had lied to her.

There was still a part of her that longed for love. For a family. For all the things she hadn't had growing up, but she just didn't see how that was possible.

"You okay?" Atticus asked, breaking through her thoughts.

"Huh?" And then she realized that they were in the air and he was speaking through the headset. "I'm okay."

"You just seemed like you were a million miles away."

I was.

"Just thinking about Sophie's biliary atresia and also wondering what the midwife would like us to do. You said that she requested us?"

He nodded. "She requested a pediatric surgeon for an opinion, but I don't know what."

"Anyways, that's what I was thinking about. The Kasai procedure and our visit to Meridian Inlet."

"Meridian Inlet is an awesome place. It's on a beautiful stretch of the northeastern arm of Great Slave Lake. I really like when I can go there. Dr. Michael Ward is an awesome general practitioner.

He's Dene and from Meridian Inlet. It's great that he chose to return home too and serve his village."

She smiled. "It's always a good thing to go home."

"Is that why you were in Calgary?" Atticus asked.

"Huh, I guess. Calgary is where I went to school, and it was close to my grandparents, who live near Black Diamond... It is home, but also not. I much prefer my grandparents' ranch in the foothills. That place felt like a real home. There was a time..." She trailed off as she thought of the brief period that her father had been with them.

Before his wife and children in India had come over. Nothing she could do would bring her father back. She'd never been good enough.

"A time?" Atticus asked.

Penny swallowed the lump in her throat. "A time when my father was still part of my life. When we had a small home in Calgary...when we were all happy. I guess that's what I associate with home or roots. Calgary is where I can advance my career. That's the most important thing now."

His expression softened, and he didn't say anything more. Penny sighed. She didn't want to think about her father or Walter or anything that revolved around feelings or the things she couldn't have.

She didn't say much more during their two-hour flight. She just spent the time watching the world below her. Great Slave Lake stretched out like a silver mirror. It was everywhere. She hadn't seen a lake so big in her life.

"There's Meridian Inlet," Atticus remarked. He began to flick switches and got a radio message from the little airstrip about where to land. The airstrip was lit up with reflective markers, and it looked like nothing more than a glorified gravel road.

The village was nestled against the shore of the lake. Brightly covered modular homes and clapboard houses clung to the lichen-covered rocks, but from the sky, she could make out the medical clinic and the RCMP station by the markings on the roof.

Kids were running down the streets as their plane flew overhead. She smiled, watching them point and speed toward the airport. There were no roads connecting Meridian Inlet to the rest of the territories, so planes and boats possibly signaled cargo and definitely let the villagers know that visitors were coming.

It was heartwarming to see.

She wasn't sure if she'd ever been in a situation where someone was excited to see her. Especially when it came to kids and doctors. It was one the harder parts of her job. She loved children so much, but they weren't always enthused to see her.

"You are clear to land aircraft Rebel One. Welcome back, Dr. Spike."

"Roger that, tower, and thanks, Peter."

Atticus landed the plane smoothly. As he brought the plane around, she could see someone was waiting in an ATV for them, and they were waving. She could only assume that was Dr. Michael Ward.

"Mike's here," Atticus remarked, confirming her suspicions. "You'll like Mike."

"I'm sure I will." She put on a brave smile, but inside she was grappling with emotions that were surprising her. Feelings of belonging and home that she thought were long buried and under control, but clearly weren't.

Ones that Atticus seemed to be stirring up.

She had to get a hold of her emotions and do her work.

That's why she was here, but she really didn't know what it was about Atticus that stirred up these feelings she realized she'd never felt for Walter. Feelings she'd never had before, with anyone. Penny didn't like losing control of herself, but when she was around him, that's exactly what happened.

It's like she forgot herself and became someone she didn't recognize.

"Mike!" Atticus called out, waving with one hand as he opened the hold on his plane. Penny reached in and grabbed her bag and a couple other bags of supplies.

Mike came over with his ATV. He parked it and got out. "I am glad to see both of you."

There was an edge to Mike's voice. Like he was

worried. It sent a shudder down her spine. There was something wrong.

Atticus and Mike shook hands. Atticus turned to her.

"Dr. Michael Ward, this is Dr. Penny Burman. Penny, this is Mike."

Mike grinned at her in a friendly way and held out his hand. "Pleasure to meet you, Dr. Burman."

"Please, call me Penny."

Mike nodded. "Will do. I never like to presume over formality, though." Mike grabbed some gear and carried it back to his ATV, which looked like a pimped-out golf cart with doors and a fancy windshield.

"So, are we going to start the wellness checks first?" Atticus asked, hefting the gear into the back of the vehicle before closing the hold.

"No. I need to take you to Martha first."

"Martha?" Penny asked. "Is that the midwife?"

Mike nodded. "Yep. She really wants to see you, Atticus, and it'll be good to have both of you there."

That sense of dread traveled down her spine, and she could see Atticus stiffen. His lips pressed together in a firm line. He was feeling it too.

"Then take us there," Atticus said.

"Yep. I was told by Martha it would mean my death if I didn't." Mike laughed nervously.

Penny climbed in the seat beside Mike, and Atticus hung onto the back.

"Can you tell us what it is?" Penny asked gently.

"Twins," Mike said. "My best guess? Conjoined twins, but it needs to be confirmed by radiologist or someone who has seen sets of conjoined twins. Someone like a surgeon."

Atticus's throat tightened, and it felt like he had a rock in his stomach when Mike mentioned conjoined twins. That's what he was famous for, separating conjoined twins.

He'd devoted years to it.

Right now, with the mention of conjoined twins, all he could see were those two little souls in Boston. He hadn't run into a set here in the Northwest Territories, and as Mike pulled up to Martha's place, he grumbled internally that it was apparently only a matter of time. Since they were at the midwife's, he was making the assumption that the twins hadn't been delivered.

So his only consolation was that he would suggest the mother be flown to a city to deal with the birth, and he wouldn't be involved other than in the diagnosis. And that's what he had to keep telling himself.

Martha met them at the door. "Atticus, so glad you came."

Atticus nodded stiffly. "Martha, this is Dr. Penny Burman. She's a pediatric surgeon from Calgary."

Martha smiled warmly. "Pleased to meet you, Penny."

"Likewise."

"I'll take your things," Mike said. "After you meet with Martha, you can just come over and we'll start the wellness clinic."

"Thanks, Mike," Atticus said.

Mike drove the supplies away.

Martha sighed. "I'm glad you're both here. I have a pregnant woman and...my little ultrasound picked up something unusual."

"Well, let's take a look," Atticus said stiffly. Dread was forming in the pit of his stomach, but he wouldn't let this stop him. This was his job; this was what he was passionate about. This was his life.

He didn't have anyone, other than his parents, Ginny's family, and Horatio in his life. He kept everyone else at arm's length, never letting them too close. This is what he was devoted to, and no amount of anxiety from his past was going to stop him from taking a look at the ultrasound.

Martha led them into her office and shut the door. "I'll bring up the images on my computer. The couple are still here. They actually don't live in Meridian Inlet proper. They live on a homestead about twenty miles from here. They're trying to live off the grid, and when she found out she was pregnant in the winter, they were stuck and had to wait to get in town."

"But it's fall," Penny stated.

"They don't have a vehicle. They walked here."

Atticus's eyes widened, and he shared that shocked look with Penny.

"Okay," he said carefully.

"They came into town because she's due soon and this is their first." Martha brought up the ultrasound. "Because she didn't have prenatal care, I decided to do an ultrasound and discovered she was carrying twins, but then I noticed this."

Atticus leaned over, to look at the ultrasound more closely, and he could see where the twins were attached. He could make out one liver. What they needed was an MRI or CT scan to show more detailed imagery, but Martha's first instincts were right.

They were conjoined twins, and if he had to guess, he would peg them as omphalopagus conjoined twins, which meant they were joined at the abdomen. There were two hearts beating and four arms and legs.

"I'm glad to see four lungs on this imagery," Atticus remarked. He leaned over her computer and zoomed in the best he could. "How far along is she?"

"Thirty weeks is my best estimate."

Atticus cocked an eyebrow. "Usually conjoined twins start to deteriorate, and they come early."

Martha nodded. "She can't have a natural birth. Not here."

"No, you're correct." Atticus scrubbed a hand

over his face. "Yellowknife isn't big enough to handle this."

"Calgary is," Penny stated. "The hospital where I work can handle a conjoined twin separation. It's been done there before. We have some of the best pediatric surgeons on staff."

Atticus's body went numb at Penny's eagerness to return to Calgary.

So eager to jump on a high-profile case. Maybe she'd even use this to go back home sooner. She didn't hide the fact she was going to return to Calgary.

That she wanted to.

"Can you contact Calgary?" Martha asked, breaking through his thoughts.

"Can we arrange a medevac flight to Calgary?" Atticus asked.

"I can arrange the medevac plane," Martha said. "Once it's firmed up Calgary can take her."

"Can I speak with the mother now?" Atticus asked.

"Yes. Please do." Martha got up and Atticus followed, while Penny made her call to Calgary.

Martha knocked on a door to one of the birthing rooms. "Georgie?"

"Come in," a voice called out.

Martha opened the door, and Atticus saw the mother in bed, looking exhausted and uncomfortable. Her husband was sitting next to her.

"Dale and Georgie, this is Dr. Atticus Spike.

He's a pediatric surgeon from Fort Little Buffalo, and he specializes in pediatric surgery and neonatology."

Dale and Georgie looked concerned.

Atticus made his way to the chair next to Georgie's bed and held out his hand. "A pleasure to meet you both."

Dale and George both shook his hand.

"Martha told me you walked here. How long did it take?"

Dale and Georgie exchanged glances. Georgie, the mother, spoke first. "A month or so. We wanted to come sooner, but we had things to do to secure our cabin, and we were trying to be mindful of bears in the area after hibernation."

"We live off the land there. We're self-sufficient, but we're just starting out. I plan to get all-terrain vehicles, and I do have my pilot's license," Dale offered, nervously.

"I'm not here to judge how you live," Atticus said calmly, "Has Martha explained what's going on?"

Georgie's eyes filled with tears. "Yes."

"You realize your twins are conjoined. I need better imaging, but I have seen many cases of conjoined twins. It appears they're joined at their abdomen. They have separate hearts, which is excellent. They share a liver, which is tricky, and because of the fact you've carried them longer than they usually stay in utero, we need to fly you down to Calgary. We need to get better imaging and a larger team to separate them if separation is what you want. If it's not, the babies can live conjoined, but it will be harder for them, and they are medically complex children. Not conducive, sadly, to your choice of life."

Dale nodded. "We understand. We would like them separated, and we understand that my wife can't have them naturally. We're more than able to go to wherever. I just want my wife and children to be safe."

Atticus smiled. "Good."

Penny knocked on the door, and Atticus motioned for her to come in. "This is Dr. Penny Burman. She's a pediatric surgeon from Calgary."

Georgie and Dale smiled, and Penny shook their hands.

"Calgary is ready," Penny stated. "As soon as we can fly them out of here, they will get the imaging they need."

"Good." Atticus stood.

Penny gave Martha the contact information for Calgary and trailed Atticus out of the patient's room.

"What's wrong?" he asked, because he could sense there was a problem.

"They want you," Penny stated. "Both of us, really. They don't have the expertise that you have, and once they learned you were here…"

"They have surgeons," Atticus said quickly.

"But these are our patients."

Atticus felt his stomach twist at how possessive she was, like staking her territory. "It'll be fine. Besides, separation doesn't happen straight after birth. It will take months."

Penny nodded. "Okay."

Atticus sighed. "You'll be back in time, and I'll of course consult with Calgary and the surgeon in charge there."

She smiled. "You will?"

"Sure." He swallowed the lump in his throat, trying to ease the sense of dread and déjà vu bothering him. "Now, let's go do what we're actually here for and run the wellness clinic. There's nothing more we can do for Georgie right now. The neonatologist team will help obstetrics deliver the babies, but we can help the kids here."

They left Martha's midwife clinic. As he stepped outside, there was a chill in the air, and there were dark clouds rolling in from Great Slave Lake to the west.

Which seemed only fitting for the storm of emotions that were eating away at him.

CHAPTER ELEVEN

ATTICUS TRIED NOT to think about the conjoined twins. Martha got them on a medevac flight, and Penny went to help Martha with transporting Georgie to the airstrip and to speak with the air paramedics about who to contact when they got to Calgary.

Penny seemed really eager about being involved in this case.

Not that he could blame her. It was a rare occurrence.

She was young and had a career ahead of her, a name to make for herself. Calgary could offer her more than Fort Little Buffalo.

He focused on the wellness checks that he was helping Mike with. He saw some of the kids that needed more specialized help than Mike could provide.

And he got to check in with a few of his regular Meridian Inlet patients.

It was good to focus on work.

It kept his mind off the twins. Off the fact that Calgary had wanted him to go down there and handle the case. There was a part of him that wanted to be involved with the twins. There were times when he genuinely missed working in a state-of-the-art facility and seeing all kinds of different patients. Having whatever he needed at his disposal.

They were few and far between, because he truly did love his life up in the north, back home and helping those who really needed it.

Penny came in the room. "The medevac got off okay."

"I suspected it would," Atticus remarked, finishing a chart for Michael.

"Did you not see the storm?"

"Storm?" Atticus asked, confused.

Penny nodded. "You've been working here in the back. A snowstorm hit. We were worried that the medevac wouldn't be able to take off, but we got Georgie loaded before the storm really hit."

Atticus rose and walked out into the clinic waiting room, where there were windows. His mouth dropped open to see the raging blizzard outside.

"I don't think we're going home tonight," Penny stated with worry.

"No. I don't think so." He ran his hand through his hair. "There isn't a hotel in Meridian Inlet."

"The RCMP's cabin is empty. We're waiting for a new constable to come, and right now it's fully furnished and waiting. You could both stay there tonight," Michael suggested.

Atticus wasn't sure about this turn of events that would have him staying in a cabin with Penny overnight, but what choice did they have?

"That sounds good. Thanks, Michael." Atticus

was trying to ignore his pulse thundering in his ears, his blood heating, and how much he wanted to be alone with Penny. He didn't need those thoughts creeping through his head at this moment.

Michael shrugged. "It's no problem. I'll make sure some food is sent, enough for you two to crash there until the storm subsides and you can fly back to Fort Little Buffalo."

"Can we make it to the cabin through the blizzard?" Penny asked.

Michael chuckled. "The community buildings are attached. So right through that door is the entrance to the police detachment, and the cabin is in the detachment. Don't worry, no one is in the drunk tank tonight."

Michael went and unlocked the door.

Penny grabbed her bag. "Well, I guess we have no choice. I really don't relish the idea of sleeping in the clinic."

"No. You're right." Atticus grabbed his bag, too, and followed her through, with Michael trailing after them.

The detachment was empty, and Michael showed them where the constable's quarters were. The cabin was sparse but furnished. There was one couch and one bed.

"It's on propane heat, So you don't even have to worry about a fire," Michael said, turning on the furnace.

"Thank you, Mike."

"No, thank you both for coming up here and helping with the wellness checks and for helping with Georgie." Michael shook his head. "I'm very glad you both came."

"You know I'll always help," Atticus remarked.

Michael nodded. "I'll go round up some grub for you two. I'll be back soon."

Michael left through the detachment, shutting the doors behind him.

It was just him and Penny, alone in the officer's quarters with just one bed.

"I'll take the couch," Penny offered. There was a hint of nervousness in her voice too. As if she was suddenly very aware of the fact there was only one bed. Was she thinking about the kiss on the beach the other day?

He was.

It was always in the back of his mind.

He vividly recalled the way she felt in his arms, the way her lips had tasted. His pulse began to race, and he had to control the desire he was feeling for her.

"No, I'll take the couch," he said gruffly. "I'm nothing but a gentleman."

Penny crossed her arms. "You're over six feet, and this is a short couch. Besides, you have to fly us back, and the last thing I want to do is fly with a pilot who is having back problems."

"Fine." He tossed his bag on the bed. He saw there was a television, an outdated VCR, and a not so huge selection of VHS movies. "Want to watch a movie tonight?"

Penny made her way over to the shelf. She was standing so close to him; he could smell her shampoo. That sweet smell he loved so much.

"It's all slasher flicks. Interesting choice for a police constable, but there are some of those academy movies? Not familiar with those."

"They're comedies. You know, the ones about the police school."

Penny wrinkled her nose. "I'd rather watch one of those B-rated horror slasher flicks."

"Come on," he teased.

She rolled her eyes. "You get the bed. I pick the movie."

He rolled his eyes, but only sarcastically. "Fine."

Penny ran her fingers over the VHS tapes and pulled out a particular bad horror movie that had aired in his youth. He visibly cringed when he saw it.

"You really want that one?" he asked.

"Yes. My choice, remember?" She made her way to the television and turned it on, making sure that the VCR was hooked up. There was a knock at the door, and Atticus made his way through the empty detachment office and opened it.

Mike was bundled up, and Martha was with him.

"Food," Martha said, holding up a bunch of covered dishes.

"That's fantastic."

Mike, Martha and couple of the other ladies brought in the dishes and made their way to the small quarters in the back and the kitchen.

"Hopefully the storm will die down tomorrow so you can both fly out," Michael said. "Pete said he'd call you the moment it's safe to fly."

"I appreciate that," Atticus said. "I have a surgery on an infant I need to complete in the next day or so."

Atticus showed everyone out and locked the detachment door and then locked the door to the RCMP quarters. He peered out of one of the windows. It seemed darkness was beginning to fall, though he couldn't really tell through the howling snow. He saw the lights of snowmobiles driving away.

"You think they'll get home okay?" Penny asked worriedly.

"Yeah, they all live close by." Atticus made his way over to the kitchen and started opening the potluck-style dinner that had been left. "There's a couple casseroles that might have beef…"

"That's okay, I'll avoid what I think might have secret beef in there. If it was venison or something, I would be fine."

Atticus leaned over. "It might be that. Or moose."

"There's fish here," Penny said excitedly. "Fried fish. I think I'll stick with that. It all smells so good."

"There's a note on this dish," Atticus remarked.

It was from Martha, who told him that none of the dishes had beef or bison. "You're safe. Fish and vegetable dishes."

Penny's eyes sparkled with excitement, and she clapped her hands. "That is so nice of them to provide meals"

"The people here are caring and generous." He pulled down two plates from the cupboards, and Penny got out utensils. "How about we eat out in the living room and watch the movie?"

"That sounds great. Just don't spill all over my bed or I'm crashing with you."

It was an innocent comment, but the thought of sharing a bed with her made his blood heat with desire. He would like to share a bed with her, to hold her in his arms all night.

To protect her.

Not that she needed him, but he still felt a desire to take care of her.

Cherish her.

It surprised him how fierce the feelings were, even though they were unwelcome for his heart, but they were also welcome, because he wanted Penny. It had been a long time since he'd wanted someone.

He hadn't been with anyone since Sasha, because he wasn't the kind of man who just slept around to scratch an itch. That wasn't him.

If he gave into what he was feeling with Penny, someone who he knew wasn't staying here, then he would be the kind of man he swore he never would be.

Right now, though, he wanted to be that man.

Even for just one night, for one chance to be with her.

Penny loaded up her plate and made her way to the couch. She set her plate down on the coffee table and sat cross-legged on the floor, her back against the couch.

He smiled, watching her.

He was falling for her, and he wasn't sure how he was going to stop himself from getting hurt or how he could ever let her go, because she'd made it clear that there was nothing in Fort Little Buffalo for her.

The food was so good, and the movie was terrible.

It was a perfect way to pass a snowstorm, and the awful movie helped her keep her mind off the fact that Atticus was sitting on the floor next to her. His arms were folded across his chest, and he scowled at the television screen in silent protest.

"You really hate this?" she asked.

"Yes. Horror is so not my thing," he grumbled.

She hit Rewind as the movie ended. "Okay, you get to watch your police comedy, then."

He cocked an eyebrow. "For real? Or are you just teasing me?"

"No. For real." She got up and took the plates to the kitchen. "If you do the dishes."

"I knew there was a catch," he muttered, standing up.

"I'll dry."

"Of course, take the easy job."

Penny chuckled softly and grabbed a towel while Atticus ran the water and filled the sink.

"You'd think the detachment would have a dishwasher," Atticus groused. "Even my cabin has a dishwasher."

"I know, it's very modern and yet rustic. I love your cabin." Penny took a cleaned plate and dried it.

"I don't live like a pioneer. I kept telling you this."

"And I've told you, when you wear those flannel shirts, you look like a mountain man or something. Besides, you cooked me dinner over a fire."

"What's wrong with my flannel? It's warm. Spider wieners are the best over the campfire."

"I've never been a fan of flannel. I don't mind the red-and-black flannel, I suppose."

"Should I take it off?" he teased, his eyes twinkling.

"What?"

He shook the water off his hands and dried them before slowly unbuttoning his flannel shirt.

Her heart began to race, her body heat rising as she watched him undo the buttons. "What're you doing?"

"You don't like the flannel, so I'm getting rid of it."

"No!" Penny reached out and stopped him, but her hand slipped into his shirt, and she made contact with the hard wall of his muscular chest. Her stomach flipped with that simple touch.

It was like a jolt of electricity coursed through her, right down to the very tips of her toes. She didn't move her hand away. She just stood there, feeling his heart beating under the palm of her hand against his bare chest.

"Penny," he whispered.

Her mouth went dry, and all she could think about was how he'd kissed her. How good he had made her feel in that one single moment. No one had ever really made her feel like that before. She might have been hurt, but that didn't mean she couldn't feel.

She met his gaze, and she was paralyzed.

She imagined what it would feel like to be in his arms. It was dangerous ground to be treading on, because she knew that she was falling for him, but she could have just one night of pleasure with him.

Maybe then she could get him out of her mind and focus on work.

Maybe then she wouldn't imagine herself staying with him, and then it wouldn't hurt so much to leave.

Even though she knew she shouldn't, she just wanted one night with Atticus. Just one night to chase away all the bad memories of betrayal from Walter. She wanted to cleanse her soul. Atticus's kiss still burned against her lips.

At the time she had pushed him away because she thought it was for the best, but now she wasn't so sure.

She wanted this moment.

Penny touched his cheek, her breathing becoming faster. She wanted him to know what she wanted. His hands brushed the hair from her face.

"Penny," he whispered huskily.

"It's okay. We don't need to make promises. We can just have tonight."

"Are you sure?"

"Yes," she answered, leaning forward to get closer to him. She pressed her lips against his, kissing him lightly. Her body trembled as she let herself just feel, just be in the moment.

So she could wipe away all the bad memories and the embarrassment of her past.

Atticus pulled her close. He undid her hair, and their kiss deepened. Her blood was thrumming through her veins, hot with need and desire.

Atticus's hands moved down her back. He broke the kiss only to scoop her up in his arms to carry her the short distance to the bed.

He set her down and she ran her hands over him, slipping her hands under his shirt, removing it and touching his skin, feeling the heat of his flesh under her fingers.

Atticus pulled her close, leaning his forehead against hers. She could feel his pulse racing, his breathing deep, just like hers.

"Are you sure you want this, Penny?"

"Do you?" she asked.

"Oh, yes."

She smiled and kissed him again. "I do too. As long as you have protection."

"I do." He cupped her face, kissing her deeply.

They quickly removed their clothes, and she was glad to. She wasn't ashamed to be naked in front of him. It just felt right, and she wanted to feel all of him.

She wanted nothing between them.

Just skin and their lips.

Atticus ran his hands through her hair.

"I have dreamed of this. You are so soft," he murmured. He brushed her hair to the side and kissed her neck, where her pulse was thrumming.

A shiver of pleasure rushed over her. He moved his hands over her body, touching every inch of her. Her nipples puckered as he cupped her breasts.

She both loved and hated this torturous touching. She just wanted them together.

As one.

He trailed his kisses lower and lower.

She reveled in the heat stirring in her blood and then remembered.

"Protection?" she asked, reminding him before

going further. Not that she wanted to stop but she wanted to be safe.

He grinned and moved over to his backpack and pulled out a box of condoms.

"You carry a box?" she teased.

"I carry them to hand them out when I fly into remote places that might not have easy access to contraception. So I'm glad to have some."

"I'm very glad you do too." Penny took the condom packet out of his hand. "I'll take care of this."

Atticus moaned as she knelt down and rolled the condom over the length of him. She liked touching him, teasing him.

"I can't stand it," he ground out.

She grinned, standing up, but still stroking him. "Good."

He pushed her back down on the bed, hovering over her. "You'll pay for that."

"Oh?" she asked.

He kissed her again, and this time his kisses continued their journey down further. His tongue touched between her legs, licking and caressing her folds. Her body burned for him to fill her. She arched against him, silently begging him with her hips.

"What do you want, Penny?" Atticus asked, teasing her with his kisses.

"You," she whispered.

Atticus settled between her thighs. His eyes locked on hers as he entered her slowly. Filling her.

She wrapped her legs around his hips, not wanting to let him go.

He thrust slowly.

Achingly so, when all she wanted was for him to take her hard and fast. She urged him on, rolling her hips. Pleasure began to unfurl in the pit of her stomach and she dug her nails into his skin, holding on as she crept closer to the edge until it washed through her.

Cleansing her.

Healing her.

She cried out. She didn't want the feeling to ever end.

Atticus quickened his pace, climaxing soon after, resting against her as he caught his breath. He rolled away, and Penny curled up beside him, listening to his heart, his breath and the howl of the storm outside.

She wished she could stay here with him forever, but she couldn't risk her heart, and he had made it clear he wasn't interested in a happily-ever-after with anyone.

So she savored this stolen moment with a man who was not meant to be hers.

Atticus wasn't sure when Penny drifted off to sleep, but he couldn't sleep. Not with her in his arms. After they cleaned up, they didn't say much, but settled in bed together. Naked, and that suited him just fine.

He was still coming down off the high of being with her and wrestling with the emotions he was feeling about making love to the most beautiful woman he had ever known. He wasn't sure what was going to happen next.

All he knew was that he was privileged to have been with her.

And he was going to enjoy lying here in the darkness in a bed, listening to the storm outside. So he didn't sleep much. He just watched her, and it took all his strength not to touch her. Not to taste her again and have her over and over like he wanted to.

Holding her was just as good.

And he was angry at himself for falling for her, because he knew that's what his traitorous heart was doing right now. He was not a one-night stand type of guy. So it wasn't a surprise that he was falling for Dr. Penny Burman, who'd made it clear that she wasn't looking for love.

Who had just gotten out of a toxic relationship and who would be leaving for Calgary at the end of her term in Fort Little Buffalo.

You could follow her, that little voice in his head suggested again.

And that thought made his anxiety spike.

The idea of going back to a big hospital and leaving everything he'd helped build up here in the north, abandoning the people, the children who relied on him, for the chance of love? It was too risky.

He had taken a gamble on love once before by staying in Boston and building a practice, and he'd lost everything because of that gamble. He couldn't gamble with the people from his home. The children who needed him.

Still, there was a part of him that wanted to take that risk.

To make that bet on love.

He reluctantly rolled over and saw that it was five in the morning. He had spent the whole night watching her, tossing, turning, and wrestling with himself. His phone lit up, and he could see that it was the airport.

"Atticus here," he answered, causing Penny to stir beside him.

"Hi, Atticus. It's Pete. You're okay to fly. Weather is clear, but there is another storm brewing."

"Okay, we'll be there in thirty minutes."

"Roger that." Pete hung up.

Atticus shook Penny gently. "Penny, we need to get up."

She muttered something into her pillow. All he could make out was that she said no. He chuckled softly to himself and shook her again.

"What?" Penny murmured. Her eyes were still closed, and her face had a crease from the pillow. She looked absolutely adorable, and all he wanted to do was spend the whole day in bed with her, but they had to get back to Fort Little Buffalo.

"It's clear to fly to Fort Little Buffalo, and we

have to get back to prep for Sophie's Kasai procedure."

That woke Penny. She sat up and rubbed her eyes, the sheet falling away to bare her breasts. His blood heated at the memory of holding them, caressing them, tasting them. He looked away quickly and got dressed, trying to ignore the fact that she was just naked in bed and now was getting dressed.

"I need coffee," she mumbled.

"There's no time and nowhere open."

"What time is it?" Penny asked.

"Five in the morning."

"How are we getting to the airport?" Penny asked.

"Mike's coming by with snowmobiles." He grabbed his bag. "I'll go first and prep the plane, and then he'll come back for you."

"What about the leftovers?"

"Martha and the other ladies will come for them. They always do."

"It was so nice of them."

An awkward tension fell between them, but he didn't know what to say. They'd both agreed that it was only one night. Neither of them was looking for anything, although there was a part of him right now that wanted more.

He just couldn't have it.

Not with her.

And he really didn't want it with anyone else.

As much as he wanted to kiss her, he didn't. He had to keep his distance from her.

"You okay?" he asked, stiffly moving away.

She smiled, still sleepy. "Fine."

"Really?"

"Yes. Go. I just really need to wake up."

He zipped up his jacket. "I'll see you in a bit."

Penny nodded.

Atticus left the cabin and walked into the snowy landscape to make his way over to Mike's. He could work with Dr. Penny Burman, but he had to keep his distance from her. He couldn't spend any extra time with her, because the more he was with her, the more he was falling in love.

Penny dozed on the flight back to Fort Little Buffalo, which was fine by Atticus. He focused on the horizon. They had chatted briefly about Sophie's surgery, until she fell asleep, and Atticus was glad for the quiet.

After they landed, he took her back to her place and then he went to his sister's to check on Horatio, shower and change to get ready for surgery. It hadn't snowed much in Fort Little Buffalo, but the temperature had dropped, and the unusual warm weather that had been there only a couple of days ago was well and truly gone.

The north was heading back into winter.

When he got to the hospital, Dr. Lance Wood

was waiting for him outside his office. Lance was pacing and looked concerned.

"Lance?" Atticus asked. "What's wrong?"

"We don't have antibiotics for surgery," Lance said.

"What?" Atticus asked.

"Our shipment has been delayed. We have enough to administer to patients, but we don't have what you need to do the biliary atresia surgery." Lance handed him a chart. "The nurses checked little Sophie. She's not doing well."

Atticus flipped through the chart, and his heart sank seeing how Sophie was failing. She needed the procedure as soon as possible.

"What's wrong?" Penny asked, coming around the corner.

Atticus handed her Sophie's chart. "We need to do the surgery."

Penny looked at the chart. "Right. When?"

"That's the thing," Lance said. "We don't have what's needed. Supplies are backlogged and have been since the disruption from the pandemic. We can't do the Kasai procedure here."

As much as he didn't want to suggest it, they had no choice. Sophie's life was on the line.

"Do you think Calgary would allow us to do the procedure?" Atticus asked. "I just need supplies and an operating room, and you have privileges."

Penny nodded. "I'll call. I know they want you

there, Atticus. I'm sure they will be accommodating."

"I'm not going to be involved with the twins," Atticus said. "That one I handed over, but I will help with Sophie there."

Lance looked confused. "Twins?"

"Conjoined twins," Penny stated. "They flew down yesterday. They haven't been born yet."

Lance's eyes widened. "Well, if you can get Sophie to Calgary, I can work on the paperwork for her parents and arrange the medevac to transport her, her parents, and you two."

Penny nodded and left to make the call.

Atticus scrubbed a hand over his face. Lance was still staring at him.

"What?" Atticus asked.

"The twins?" Lance asked.

"Calgary took them, but wanted me to join their team."

Lance bit his bottom lip. "You want to join them?"

"No."

Lance clapped a hand on Atticus's shoulder. "You are an amazing neonatologist who has helped build this place. I would hate to lose you. We'd suffer for it. But also, you're talented."

"Don't worry," Attics stated. "This is my home."

Lance nodded. "I won't be mad either way. Just so you know. I'll start on all that paperwork to have Sophie sent to Calgary. You and Penny better get ready for a trip to Calgary. I know you both just got back from Fort Little Buffalo, but this little one needs surgery."

Atticus nodded. "Thanks, Lance."

As much as he didn't want to be alone with Penny, Sophie needed him.

He was concerned about going to this bigger hospital that kept requesting him, but it would only be for a few days at the most. Then he could come home to the north.

To where his heart was safe.

CHAPTER TWELVE

PENNY COULDN'T QUITE believe they were flying back to Calgary. She wasn't sure how long they would be there, but at least she had her place for them to crash in. She wasn't going to let Atticus stay in a hotel, not after he had been so generous and kind to her.

Of course, when she pictured him in her apartment, all she could think about was their night together in Meridian Inlet.

It was only one night. They'd agreed to that, even if she wanted more.

But she knew she couldn't have more, because there was a part of her that wasn't sure she wanted to risk her heart again.

Penny just wasn't sure that a happily-ever-after was for her.

No matter how she had melted in Atticus's arms.

Her cheeks began to flush, and she tried to get comfortable in the back of the medevac plane. She opened one eye and saw that Atticus was monitoring Baby Sophie. The baby's parents were across from him, looking apprehensive.

Not that she could blame them.

It was a tight ride in the small Medevac, but they

needed to get Sophie into surgery as fast as possible or she would die.

Penny was also worried about returning to the place where she had been disgraced, and she tried not to think of Walter or his wife. How she'd demanded that Penny be sent away or she'd take away the substantial money she'd promised to donate.

Penny was actually surprised that Calgary was okay with her coming back, but maybe it was because she was working with Atticus.

It worried her to think that Atticus would assume she was using him.

She wasn't.

All this trip meant was that she was going home, even if for a short time to work on Sophie.

Maybe they'll take you back?

And that thought wasn't as exciting as it once was. Penny crushed that idea as the pilot told them to fasten their seat belts for landing. The ambulance was waiting with a shuttle for Sophie's parents. She and Atticus were going to ride in the ambulance to the hospital. They already had clearance to begin the surgery right away.

The plane landed, and there was a flurry of activity as they prepared the incubator to transfer Sophie into the back of the waiting ambulance. Penny made sure there were warm coverings over the incubator to protect Sophie from the temperature change from the airplane to outside.

No one said much as Sophie's incubator was secured in the ambulance. Penny strapped herself in, and Atticus sat next to her.

"You okay?" he asked gently.

"I'm fine. I just want to get into surgery and give her a fighting chance."

Which was true.

"Agreed."

Penny wanted to lean her head against Atticus, but that was too intimate. This wasn't the time or place for any kind of thoughts like that. She was annoyed that she was letting these feelings control her when now was the time to focus on her work.

Sophie was all that mattered.

The ambulance was cleared to leave, and the lights came on. Penny gripped the bench as the ambulance sped away from the airport toward the hospital. With the lights and siren, it was a quick ride.

She didn't even have time to process that she was back in her home hospital. Her number one priority was Sophie as they wheeled the infant off the ambulance and into triage.

"Penny!" a friendly voice said as they made their way into the pediatric triage so she could be sent up to preoperative.

"Hi, Jill," Penny said breathlessly.

"I was wondering if you were going to be part of the transfer," Jill, the triage nurse, said pleasantly.

"Yep. I am." Penny and Jill exchanged information.

"What operating room are we using?" Atticus asked, signing papers as the triage team got Sophie up to pediatric preoperative.

"Three," Jill said. "Penny can show you where to store your stuff and change."

"Thanks, Jill," Penny said, trying not to sound too exhausted.

Atticus followed Penny as she made her way out of the triage area and up to where the surgeons got ready for the operations. They found lockers to stash their gear in, and Penny handed over scrubs.

Atticus took the scrubs and began to pull off his clothes in the locker room to change. She tried not to watch him.

One night. They'd agreed to keep things professional.

"I'll be back," she said, tearing her gaze away.

She just needed a moment to catch her breath.

Atticus was tired but so ready to do this surgery and get back home to Fort Little Buffalo.

"Well, if it isn't Dr. Spike!"

Atticus's spine straightened. "Yes."

"Dr. Duncan. Walter Duncan. It's a pleasure to see you again. We met briefly in Boston."

So this was Penny's ex. The pit of Atticus's stomach knotted. "Is that so?"

Walter's eyes narrowed. "When Dr. Burman mentioned she was working with you in Fort Little Buffalo of all places, we knew she would convince you to join us."

Atticus felt his blood go cold.

Convince me to join them?

"What do you mean?" Atticus asked carefully.

"The board would like you to join us here in Calgary, Dr. Spike, and Penny can come back too—that is, if you return."

Atticus didn't respond. All he felt was betrayal.

So that's why she was so determined to come to Calgary over another city to do the surgery.

He felt used.

He knew Penny was too good to be true. She was career-driven, just like Sasha.

She had made it clear she wanted to return to Calgary, that it was her home, so he shouldn't be surprised by this revelation.

It still hurt though.

"So let me be the first to welcome you." Walter extended his hand.

Atticus glared at it. "Excuse me. I have a surgery to attend."

"The OR is ready..." Penny stopped in her tracks. Her body froze at the sight of Walter.

"Welcome back, Dr. Burman," Walter said.

"Dr. Duncan," she responded stiffly.

"I was told you were coming back, although I'm surprised you didn't come back for the delivery of the conjoined twins. The girls were born yesterday. It made the news."

"Did it?" Penny asked.

Atticus noticed a quick uptick of excitement in her voice.

"Well, we have a surgery to attend to, don't we, Dr. Burman?" Atticus stated, not looking at Penny or her ex.

"We do," Penny said, tying on her surgical cap. She side-stepped Walter and walked with Atticus out of the locker room. "You okay?"

"Fine," he replied coldly.

It was a lie.

He wasn't okay, but there was no time to focus on that. Right now, he had a life to save.

A job to do.

One that he planned to do well, and once that was done, he'd head back home where he belonged.

Operating with Atticus was so easy.

It was like it was supposed to be.

They were supposed to be partners in tandem.

Atticus had her make the Roux-en-Y, which took little Sophie's small intestine and attached it to the liver to create a bile duct.

They removed the tiny gallbladder and made sure the affected ducts wouldn't cause a rupture. Atticus might have seemed like a big brute when she first ran into him, but watching him firsthand in surgery, working on a tiny human, was something to behold. He was gentle and precise.

"Suction please," Atticus said.

A scrub nurse leaned in removed the fluid from his operating field.

"The sutures look fantastic, Dr. Spike," Penny remarked.

"Thank you. It should hold. I think this procedure will work well. We'll have to monitor her for a few days to make sure that the new duct is working. There's always a risk of failure," Atticus stated, finishing the procedure.

Penny nodded. "She'll still have some hard work to heal."

Atticus glanced up at her, but his eyes were hardened. It threw her off guard. It stung. Something had changed, but she wasn't sure what.

"I think that should about do it," Atticus remarked. "Dr. Fellowes, would you close up our patient?"

The resident in the operating room stepped forward, eagerly. "Gladly, Dr. Spike."

Calgary was excited Atticus was here, but Penny could tell Atticus was uncomfortable. He was quieter than usual. His body was stiff and not relaxed.

"I want to be informed of any postoperative changes by the pediatric critical care unit," Penny said, stepping away from Sophie's tiny body.

"Yes, Dr. Burman," Dr. Fellowes said.

Penny and Atticus headed into the scrub room, peeling off their gowns and gloves. The water felt good. Her arms were aching, and she was still so tired from their time in Meridian Inlet. She glanced up at the clock on the wall; it was seven in the evening.

"Do you think there's an on-call room I can crash in?" Atticus asked, stifling a yawn as he scrubbed his hands and forearms.

"There's my place."

A strange look passed over his face. "I thought it was a one-time thing…"

It hurt to hear him say that, but what did she expect? It *was* a one-time thing, and she wasn't looking for a relationship.

"I have an extra bed for when my half sister visits. You can crash there."

"Oh." He sounded odd. "Sure."

Penny dried her hands, but couldn't shake the feeling something was wrong. "I'll meet you in the main lobby in twenty minutes?"

Atticus nodded. "Sure."

She smiled weakly. "Okay then."

She exited the scrub room. It had hurt when he'd reminded her that their night together was a one-off.

Isn't that what you wanted?

The thing was, she didn't know what she wanted, and her heart was confused about what to do. She was angry at herself for falling for a man who was off limits. A man who had closed himself off to her with no explanation.

* * *

Atticus didn't want to go to Penny's, but he needed to talk to her about what Walter had said. It was eating away at him.

He had to remind himself that she was just inviting him to her apartment because they were stuck here in Calgary for a couple of days while Sophie recuperated.

Penny and he both wanted to watch Sophie for the first forty-eight hours after the Kasai procedure to make sure that the new ducts were working and the bile was flowing correctly from the liver.

He could've let the surgeons here monitor Sophie, but he wanted to make sure.

It was a bit unnerving being back in a big hospital.

It was warmer in Calgary. It had been some time since he'd been south.

"Do we need to get a cab?" Atticus asked.

"Nope, we can walk. I don't live too far away. Not in the woods like you," she teased.

He laughed, relaxing a bit. "The city is a different kind of monster."

"It is, but here at this hospital, it is so nice to have everything on hand," she said enthusiastically.

It made his stomach turn, because it was the truth.

"Yes," he said quietly. He understood her point, but in Fort Little Buffalo, there wasn't a game of politics. He knew everyone. Here Penny would be a faceless cog. Up north, she wouldn't be just a shadow.

She'd matter. Why couldn't she see that?

She was chatting as they navigated the streets. He was half listening to her. It was apparent that Penny loved it here. So much so that she was using him as a way to come back sooner?

He couldn't stay here. He wouldn't fall for someone who only used him for fame. For his name.

He just couldn't.

Atticus stopped. "I forgot something at the hospital."

Penny looked confused. "Oh?"

"Yeah. I think I'll crash there anyways. I can keep a closer eye on Sophie."

Penny looked stunned, and he hated lying to her, but it was easier to lie and put this separation between them. Atticus had no doubt Calgary would want her back right away, and she would stay. With or without him.

Fort Little Buffalo had nothing to offer her. Sasha had told him the same. It would kill him to hear it from Penny.

He returned to the hospital.

And as he walked through the halls towards to the pediatric critical care unit, he could feel people were watching him. They were looking at him differently, because they knew who he was. The world-class neonatal surgeon from Boston who'd disappeared five years ago. Although he hadn't disappeared in Fort Little Buffalo. It's just that it was under the radar for everyone who thought only city surgeons mattered.

Word was spreading like wildfire through the hospital.

It was unnerving. He was regretting his decision to return here for the night.

"Dr. Spike, could I get a moment of your time?"

Atticus groaned inwardly and turned to see another surgeon racing toward him.

"Sure," Atticus said through gritted teeth.

The middle-aged man held out his hand. "I'm Dr. Tom Greene and I'm the head of neonatology here. It's a pleasure to meet you."

"The pleasure is all mine. How can I help you, Dr. Greene?"

"I have a BPS case."

"Bronchopulmonary sequestration?" Atticus asked.

Dr. Greene handed him a tablet and loaded some images. "The fetus is about twenty-nine weeks. He can be delivered if need be. You can see the fluid building around the heart and that the mass is growing. The baby won't survive, and the mother's blood pressure is being affected. You have done this fetal surgery before, and I thought you could help?"

Atticus flicked through the images. "Twenty-nine weeks?"

Dr. Greene nodded. "I have done BPS surgeries

on neonates, but I have not done a fetal surgery. I was preparing the mother to airlift her to Vancouver or Toronto, but since you're here…"

"I can do it. Tonight, in fact. If the mother's blood pressure is rising, we need to get a shunt in the baby's chest to divert the fluid into the amniotic fluid. The BPS can then be repaired when you deliver the baby at term."

"That is my plan," Dr. Greene said excitedly. "The patient will be pleased not to be airlifted away from Calgary and her family."

Atticus glanced at his watch. "I'll meet you on the operating room floor?"

Dr. Greene nodded. "Thank you. Do you mind the gallery being used?"

A pit of dread formed in Atticus's stomach. "The gallery?"

Did Penny suggest this too? Another way to butter up the board of directors?

"We have an awful lot of residents and interns who would love to watch you work and to see a fetal surgery."

He should say no, but he was in debt to the hospital for allowing him to work on Sophie and for taking the conjoined twins off his hands. He nodded.

"Fantastic. I will meet you in an hour." Dr. Greene scurried away.

Atticus groaned inwardly.

He hated the idea of all those eyes on him, but this was a teaching hospital, and there had been a time in his life when he'd liked teaching others. He liked sharing his knowledge. After what happened in Boston, when he started losing patients because of bad press, no one wanted to hear what he had to say.

Speaking engagements were dropped.

He was no longer a teacher, and that had hurt too.

It worried him, but he was glad to be of help. For a patient's sake, for the sake of a child.

Penny was confused by Atticus suddenly changing his mind and heading back to the hospital. She thought that was the last place he'd want to go. It was a bit weird being back in her apartment. Not that she spent a lot of time here. It wasn't really home.

It hit her that no place really felt that way.

When she unlocked the door, she could hear music, and as she entered her apartment, she saw her half sister, Priyah, was curled up on the couch.

"Priyah?" Penny asked.

Priyah jumped up. "Oh, my goodness! I had no idea you were back in town."

Penny hugged a very excited Priyah.

"What're you doing here?" Penny asked, stunned.

"Don't be mad. I needed a quiet place to study, and the dorm is so loud. I had your key. I've only been here a couple of days."

"No, I'm not mad." Penny set down her bag. "I'm really glad to see you. I've missed you."

Priyah sat on the couch and patted a cushion. "Come tell me about the north!"

"There's nothing to tell..."

"Really? Have you told your mom the reason you went there?"

Penny groaned, regretting telling Priyah about Walter just before she'd left. "I hate you see through me."

"I take it you haven't talked to her. You should."

Penny scrubbed her hand over her face. "I'm really tired, and I need a shower."

Priyah scooted away laughing at Penny's needing a shower remark. Penny just shook her head as her phone buzzed. It was Walter.

She was going to ignore it until she read that Atticus was doing a BPS surgery on a fetus. She didn't respond, but got up and grabbed her purse; she had to see this surgery.

"Where are you going?" Priyah asked.

"Back to the hospital. There's a once-in-a-life-time fetal surgery being done by a..." She swallowed the lump in her throat. She didn't want Priyah to know about Atticus and how she was falling for him. Especially since Atticus had seemed to have thrown a wall up since their night together. "A surgeon who is top in his field."

"Okay. Have...fun?" Priyah said brightly.

Penny nodded. "I'll be back later."

Penny walked quickly to the hospital. She made her way to the operating room floor, running right into Atticus, who seemed surprised that she was there.

"There's a BPS surgery, but it has to be done in utero, and your hospital is currently without a fetal surgeon," he stated awkwardly.

"That's exciting!" she said. "Walter texted me to let me know."

A strange expression crossed his face. "He texted you."

"Yes."

"He's opening the gallery if you want to stay and watch."

"When is this happening?"

"Soon, I'm on my way to the operating room," he said stiffly. Not looking at her.

Penny nodded. "Okay, then I'm headed to the gallery to get a good seat. You sure you're okay with this?"

"Why wouldn't I be?" he snapped.

It hurt how he spoke to her. Maybe it was just nerves?

"I know you're not a fan of big hospitals," she said.

She wanted to reach out and hug him, reassure him that having an audience would be okay.

This wasn't Boston.

And no one blamed him. It hadn't been his fault.

He was talented, and this was his chance to show everyone that.

"It's okay." Only he didn't seem to be okay. More annoyed? With her?

"Well, you'd better get back to the operating room."

Atticus *was* slightly nervous, but not because of the surgery, though it had been five years since he had placed a shunt in a fetus. Here in Calgary he would be well looked after. He would never even attempt this kind of surgery in Fort Little Buffalo, not that he came across many cases up there.

What was making him nervous was the gallery. The very full gallery. He could see them through the scrub room. It was standing room only.

There were plenty of times in the past when he would pack a gallery, but after the tragedy with the twins in Boston, his galleries soon emptied. When the world that had once wanted him so badly no longer trusted him.

They'd rejected him.

Just like Sasha had done.

Penny is there.

Seeing her in the gallery made him smile, but only for a moment as he remembered what Walter had told him.

He'd thought she didn't just want to be around him because of his fame. Now he wasn't so sure.

She was only here at this moment because Walter had told her about it. He ignored that creeping moment of self-doubt. There was no place for it here. He couldn't let it worm its way in right now. He was very familiar with BPS, though it was mostly performed after delivery. He was very good at shunt placements.

He had written several award-winning papers on it.

"So you're doing the shunt, are you?"

Atticus turned to see Walter had come into the scrub room. The man was handsome, clean-cut, and was oozing confidence. Or maybe ego.

"I am," Atticus replied quickly.

"I am the cardiothoracic surgeon here. I place shunts all the time."

"After delivery, yes. I know, but you have no experience in fetal surgery, or am I mistaken?" Atticus asked.

Walter frowned. "You are not mistaken, but I'm sure that I could do it. Just ask Penny."

Arrogance, not ego. That's the word he was looking for, and a flash of jealously rushed through him at the mention of Penny.

"Well, I have done this procedure many times."

"Really? What about in the last five years since you put your tail between your legs and hightailed it to the land of ice and snow?"

Atticus's spine hardened, and he saw red. "I beg your pardon?"

Walter grinned and then nodded in the direction of the gallery. "I see you've formed a friendship with Dr. Burman. She likes famous surgeons. Doesn't care if they're married or not, as long as they have something she needs. Very similar to her mother."

It took every ounce for Atticus not to strike him, but he had to be careful of his hands. The last thing he needed in this moment was his knuckles to swell so he would be unable to perform the surgery.

"You need to leave my operating room now before I have you removed," Atticus said dangerously. "I can take care of the shunt. You're not needed here." He finished scrubbing up and entered the operating room. He glanced up at Penny, his blood still burning with rage as she smiled down at him.

Sasha had only been with him because of the fame he brought, but Penny was different. He knew that.

How do you know?

Penny was still texting Walter. Penny was clearly happy here.

Atticus shook that horrible thought away.

He had a surgery to do.

A tiny life, so fragile, was in need of his help.

Penny stood in the gallery watching Atticus in his element. This was a dream come true, watching him do a fetal surgery. He was well-known for his success with separating conjoined twins—that is what made him world-famous—but there had been this side to him too.

The brilliant fetal surgeon.

And after watching him firsthand during Sophie's surgery and seeing him with his patients, she understood how amazing he really was. How gentle he was with the tiniest of patients. And this patient was indeed the smallest she had ever seen him work on.

The patient was still in utero.

The mother was awake, it was better for the baby. The mother felt nothing, having been given an epidural. The mother was draped, and a nurse sat with her, talking with her as Dr. Greene and Atticus used an ultrasound to guide a hollow needle known as a trocar through mother's abdomen and into the baby. The shunt then would be placed through the needle and into the baby.

Once the baby was stronger and could be delivered, they would repair the mass of lesions that was growing in the lungs.

"Penny," Walter said from behind her.

She froze just hearing his voice again.

Before, she would've loved to hear him whisper her name, but now she was just annoyed that he was standing so close to her, interrupting her thoughts.

"Walter," she said, barely glancing at him.

"Can we talk?" Walter asked.

She rolled her eyes. "I don't think we have anything to talk about."

"Please. You saw my text. Obviously, because you're here."

Others in the gallery were turning to look at them, and Penny was embarrassed. She nodded and followed Walter out of the gallery. She shut the door, and it was just the two of them in the hallway.

"What do you want, Walter?" Penny asked. "Why are you emailing me? I don't think your wife would like that very much."

"She left me," Walter said.

Penny's heart skipped a beat. A month ago, she would have been thrilled to hear that, to think that she and Walter would've had a chance, but instead she felt nothing. Just dread.

"Are you surprised?" Penny asked.

"That's kind of heartless," he snarled.

"What do you expect, Walter? Seriously? You broke my heart, and I had to leave Calgary because your wife couldn't stand having me work in the same hospital as you."

Walter sighed. "I know, but that's all changed."

"Has it?"

"It has. I want you back. Why do you think I've been emailing and texting? I don't need your help. I want *you*. What we had. We could be great together."

Those were the words that she'd thought she wanted to hear, that he wanted her back when she first left, but now she didn't care. They were without meaning.

Not since meeting Atticus.

Those were the words that her mother had always wanted to hear from her father, but never did.

Her mother had never stopped loving her father. Never given up on the hope that he would come back. There had been a fraction of time that Penny had secretly hoped Walter would utter those words, but now she couldn't care less that he was saying the things she'd once wanted him to say.

"I don't want you," Penny told him.

Walter's expression hardened. "You're waiting for Dr. Spike? I get why you brought him here, so you could return, but you really think he'll date you once he gets here?"

She could feel the flush in her neck as it crept up to her cheeks. "What?"

"I guessed right. You only chase those who can further your career. Just like my wife said."

Penny glared at Walter. "Keep away from me."

She stormed off, tears in her eyes. She'd been a fool to think that she was in love with Walter. She clearly didn't know what love was supposed to be, and this just reaffirmed her suspicions that love wasn't for her.

She found herself in the pediatric critical care unit. She'd check on Sophie, because doing her work always calmed her, and Sophie was her patient. Penny slipped on a white lab coat and made her way into the unit, greeting all the interns and nurses she knew so well.

Sophie's Isolette was in the corner, and Penny made her way there.

Sophie's mother was sleeping next to the Isolette. Penny didn't want to disturb her. She picked up Sophie's chart and was pleased with the numbers. The Kasai procedure was working so far. Penny replaced the chart and then caught sight of Georgie and Dale from Meridian Inlet in the next room.

Georgie was in a gown, in a wheelchair, and the babies were on an infant warmer.

Penny gently rapped on the door. "Georgie and Dale, I just wanted to congratulate you both on your baby girls. I heard they were born."

"Thank you." Dale smiled. "Dr. Burman, what're you doing here?"

"We thought you were back in Fort Little Buffalo," Georgie said.

"Dr. Spike and I had to fly to Calgary for one of our patients who needed a complicated surgery." Penny made her way over to the infant warmer and peered over at the tiny omphalopagus twin girls. "They're beautiful."

Georgie smiled, pleased. "The doctors were shocked I'd carried them for so long."

"So was I," Penny said gently. "May I look at their chart?"

"Of course," Dale said. "When it's safe, we'll go

ahead and get them separated, and we would very much like you and Dr. Spike to be a part of it."

"We trust both of you," Georgie said. "You two were so kind. Everyone here is so rushed."

Penny nodded. "It's a little more laid back in the north, for sure. What are their names?"

"Jasmine and Jenny," Dale said. "We each named one."

Penny smiled. "That's so nice."

She flipped through the chart and saw all the images that had been made of the girls since they were born. Atticus was right, they didn't share a heart and it appeared they only shared a liver, but as she was scrolling through the images, she saw figures and an image that disturbed her.

The little girl on the left, Jasmine, had gas in her bowels. That wasn't unusual, except for the amount and the fact that it was streaky-looking. Penny set the chart down and then examined Jasmine's stomach. There was some redness that was hard to see because of where the twins were joined.

"Is everything okay, Dr. Burman?" Georgie asked.

"I think so, but I want something checked out if that's okay? I'm going to ask Dr. Spike when he gets out of his surgery to confer."

Georgie nodded. "Of course."

"Try not to worry," Penny said. "Get some rest. You've been through a lot too."

Penny left their room and found the nurse in charge of the twins.

"Lily, can you tell me what the blood pressure of the conjoined twin Jasmine has been like?"

"Weak," Lily stated. "The pediatrician in charge of their delivery, Dr. Wright, has me monitoring, but she's been running a low-grade fever, and there was some green vomit."

"Bile?" Penny asked.

"Yes," the nurse said. "Just happened an hour ago after their feeding."

Penny worried her bottom lip. "Dr. Spike and I are going to take over this case."

Lily's eyes widened. "Was that cleared?"

"I'll get it cleared. Dr. Spike is the foremost neonatal surgeon and has worked with conjoined twins more than Dr. Wright. Besides, they're from the Northwest Territories. It was Dr. Spike and I who sent them here."

Lily nodded. "That's right. It's in their file."

"Inform me if Jasmine or Jenny becomes bradycardic. I need to speak to Dr. Spike."

"I will, Dr. Burman," Lily said.

Penny left the pediatric critical care unit and made her way back to the operating room floor. She had to find Atticus and talk to him about the possibility that Jasmine had developed necrotizing enterocolitis.

Usually, twin separation didn't happen until the babies were close to a year old, but if Jasmine had developed necrotizing enterocolitis, it put both babies at risk.

It could kill them both.

Penny found Atticus after he came out of the scrub room. He was chatting with Dr. Greene and then turned to look at her. His expression was unreadable as he came over to her. She was worried that something bad had happened in surgery.

"How did the operation go?" she asked.

"Textbook. We'll monitor the mother and the baby. Hopefully we can keep the baby in utero just a bit longer. You left," he said. "With Walter."

"I had a run-in with him, but that's not why I've come to talk to you."

Atticus crossed his arms. "Oh?"

"The conjoined twins."

He frowned. "They're not my patients."

"Georgie and Dale want us on the case, and I think you're going to possibly want to separate them sooner rather than later."

"Why, because the parents want it? That's not how we do things."

"No," Penny said, annoyed by his defensive attitude. "I think one of the twins is developing NEC."

Atticus's eyes widened. "What makes you think that?"

"There were streaks in the baby's intestines, redness of her belly, and the charge nurse in the pediatric critical care unit told me she threw up bile."

"I need to see the babies right away."

Penny nodded. "I can take you there now."

Atticus followed her from the operating room to the pediatric critical care unit. They didn't say anything as they walked quickly.

They entered the pediatric critical care unit.

Georgie and Dale had gone back to Georgie's room. Penny showed him where the twins were and then handed him the chart with all the images that were taken.

Atticus frowned as he flipped through the images.

"Has the baby been bradycardic?" Atticus asked.

"Lily, the nurse, hasn't said so, but you can see she has a low-grade fever." Penny motioned for Lily to come in the room.

"How's their heart rate?"

"Jenny's is fine, but Jasmine is slowing down," Lily said. "I was about to page Dr. Wright, but if you and Dr. Burman were their original doctors from up north, then I can keep you informed. I know you both have privileges since coming here."

Atticus frowned. "I suppose we are. Could you let Dr. Wright know what's happening and that I suspect NEC in little Jasmine?"

Lily nodded. "Of course. What tests would you like done?"

"I need some more imaging, and I want to check their hearts. I also want to see if there's a hole in their intestines, so I need to draw some fluid out and see if it's leaked into her abdomen."

"I can do that," Penny stated. "I've done that on infants before."

"Good," Atticus said. "I'm going to go talk to the parents, and I think I'll stay here tonight. I would like to get all the tests done as quickly as possible, because I may need to separate these babies in the morning."

"As you wish, Dr. Spike," Lily said, moving away to prep for tests.

"I know you didn't want to be involved with their case," Penny said.

"I didn't." Atticus sighed. "But you're right about what you thought it was and I think it's necrotizing enterocolitis too. Separation of twins this early is tricky, but I have done it early like this. I can repair the NEC once the twins are separated. I will need your help. I'll need Walter's help as well. It's all-hands-on-deck."

"I'll make sure the appropriate staff knows."

Atticus nodded. "I'm off to find an on-call room to study the imaging of their shared liver."

"I'll find you once I have the results."

Atticus nodded again, not saying much to her as he left the pediatric critical care unit. She knew that he was probably worried after what happened in Boston, but that hadn't been his fault. However, the publicity department at the hospital would get word that he was on the case, and the world would soon learn that Dr. Spike had resurfaced.

She just hoped that she hadn't overstepped her bounds with him.

That he forgave her for thrusting him into the limelight once more.

Atticus eventually fell asleep in an on-call room from sheer exhaustion. He had been staring at Jasmine and Jenny's scans. He fell asleep soon after the updated images hit the chart and Penny confirmed that there was a hole in Jasmine's intestines.

The babies had to be separated or they would both die.

Penny had got consent from the worried parents.

He knew she wanted to be on the case. It would be a high-profile one.

It would help advance her career.

She'd wanted to be on the case since Meridian Inlet. He would help, but he wasn't taking a permanent post for her or anyone else.

Atticus felt his stomach knot. He'd thought Penny was different. He didn't know why he'd thought that. He scrubbed his hand over his face. He needed some more sleep. At ten in the morning, there was going to be a meeting with the other staff who would be involved in the surgery.

The team at Calgary was capable, but it was always a worry.

Atticus found a clean pair of scrubs when he got up, and he cleaned himself up in the attendings' bathroom so he wouldn't look like a total wreck when he met with the other surgeons.

As much as he didn't want Walter on this case, Atticus could put personal issues aside and work with the man, even if he did want to clock him.

It had physically hurt when he saw Walter approach Penny in the gallery and he saw her leave with him. Atticus had been bothered by that, and his reaction made him so mad. Penny wasn't his.

They'd had one night together.

That was it.

Penny was returning to Calgary, and he was staying put in Fort Little Buffalo.

Focus.

And he had to keep reminding himself to do just that. It had been some time since he worked with a large team in a world class children's hospital like this. He had to remember how and not let it rattle him.

Atticus straightened the white jacket he'd been given and ran his fingers through his hair. Penny was waiting in the attendings' lounge when he came out of the bathroom. Her hair was braided and tied back in a bun, like she always wore it for work. She looked so good in the dark blue scrubs of Calgary, but she looked good in the green scrubs of Fort Little Buffalo too.

"You ready?" she asked.

"Are you?"

Penny nodded. "I'm ready. I won't lie. This has

always been a dream of mine, to work with you on a case like this."

"I'm flattered." Only he wasn't. He still felt unease. He couldn't trust her intentions.

They walked side by side down the hall toward the meeting hall where the team of surgeons, nurses, residents, interns and anesthesiologists was waiting to go over a plan of attack. They had to prep for the surgery tonight.

And he had been assured that there were suitable simulations available.

It was going to be a tricky procedure, and it had been a long time since he had led a complicated surgery like this.

Atticus entered the room, and there was a simulation set up.

"Good morning, everyone. Thank you for coming," Atticus stated as he moved to the podium. Penny stood at the back of the crowd.

"Dr. Spike, why are we separating the twins so early?" a nurse asked.

"NEC, also known as necrotizing enterocolitis. The left twin, Jasmine, has a hole in her intestines. If we don't repair this quickly, there will be tissue death and eventually the death of Jasmine." Atticus brought up the scans. "Because the twins share a liver, there is a high chance of the inflammation spreading to the right twin, Jenny. Jenny's heart has a small atrial septal defect, and scans this morning showed that her heart is working harder as the infection is taking over Jasmine. We need to separate the twins now."

"What is the plan?" Dr. Greene asked.

"I am going to work on separating the liver with you, Dr. Greene and Dr. Burman. Once the twins are separated, Dr. Burman and Dr. Duncan can repair the atrial septal defect on Jenny. Dr. Greene, you and I will repair the necrotizing enterocolitis in Jasmine. We'll be split up in teams. Team one and team two. Corresponding staff will be assigned to each twin, and we will wear numbers on our scrub caps so we know what twin we're working on."

Walter raised his hand. "What if the atrial septal defect doesn't need to be closed? Some ASDs don't require repair."

"That is for you to determine, Dr. Duncan," Atticus replied carefully. "If the atrial septal defect doesn't need to be repaired, Jenny will still need to have work done to make sure her half of the liver is functioning well. Dr. Burman worked with me on a biliary atresia case on an infant who was only fourteen days old. She's quite capable of liver resection and repair."

Walter didn't say anything further, but he could tell that Penny was annoyed to be working with Walter. Atticus knew that she wouldn't let those feelings get in the way of her work. He was so confident in her.

He trusted her surgical skills.

The idea of trusting her shocked him, because

it had been so long since he had trusted someone. Although this wasn't trusting her with his emotions. This was with an operation. He could trust her surgical abilities.

This was work.

This wasn't love.

Isn't it?

Atticus ignored that little voice in his head.

"You all have your duties, and I will remain here for the next hour to go over the procedure, but we need to start antibiotics and get the twins ready for pre-op."

The crowd dispersed, and he took a deep breath. It was the start of a long day, and he was more than ready to get this operation over and done with, so he could return home where he belonged.

CHAPTER THIRTEEN

PENNY TOOK A deep breath.

She hadn't been involved in many conjoined twin surgeries—she had always been on the periphery—but now, standing in the operating room as the scrub nurse helped her on with her gown, her heart was racing.

She reminded herself that she'd done liver resections and worked on the tiniest lives, but the gallery was full.

It had been hard to take the twins out of the pediatric preoperative area and away from Georgie and Dale, who were beyond terrified.

The hardest part of her job was that she couldn't promise parents anything, and it broke her heart seeing them so worried.

If she had her own children, she would be sick with worry too.

Only, that wasn't going to happen for her, and she knew she couldn't raise a child on her own. That was her choice. She knew amazing women and men who were single parents, but when she was young, watching her mother struggle, she just couldn't imagine doing it.

The way her life was going, she seriously doubted that a family would ever happen. Especially since she was falling so helplessly in love with a man who didn't want her.

Atticus was on the left side of the operating table, standing over little Jasmine, who was being prepped to be put under anesthesia. The twins were spread out on two gurneys so they could be separated. There was another operating room next door where little Jenny, her charge, would be whisked away after the separation.

The color red and the number two were fastened to Penny's face shield.

She took another deep breath and made her way to the operating table.

The images were being brought up on the monitors, and the lights were being adjusted.

"Dr. Spike, the twins are under anesthesia," the anesthesiologist said.

"Very well. Are we ready? We'll make a midline incision to expose the liver, and we'll begin resection to separate the twins. Scalpel please." Atticus held out his hand as the scrub nurse handed him the scalpel.

Penny watched him, holding her breath and the clamps as they worked over the liver, making sure that both twins had what they needed to survive.

She wasn't sure how long she stood there, but she drank it all in, learning from a master as Atticus worked on such small organs.

Those large hands of his moved with grace and skill.

Those same hands that had tenderly touched her.

"Ready for separation?" Atticus asked, setting his tools down. "Make sure that all the cords and monitors are out of the way. Team two, you're going to move Jenny to the next operating room, and team one, we're going to repair the intestines."

"Ready, Dr. Spike," Penny stated.

Atticus held her gaze, and it was calming. "One, two, three."

There was a flurry of activity as open wounds were covered and cords and tubes were held back. The gurneys were parted, and Penny watched the monitors with bated breath, hoping that the babies remained stable.

There was only a slight blip, but their heart rates and blood pressures were stable.

She breathed a sigh of relief and as she listened to the round of applause that could be heard from the gallery.

"Well done, everyone!" Dr. Greene said loudly over the din.

"Let's get a move on," Walter said quietly.

Penny took one last look at Atticus, who was working hard over little Jasmine to save her life. Her heart swelled watching him. She was in love with him. How could she not be?

It had nothing to do with his name or his abilities, but the fact she'd been missing him her whole life. She knew that now; he was the missing piece.

She wished she could have him and his heart wasn't so hardened by love.

Penny's back was aching, as were her feet, as she wheeled little Jenny into the pediatric postoperative care unit. The atrial septal defect was larger than anticipated, probably strained from her twin's rapid decline from the necrotizing enterocolitis, so Walter had had to repair the hole in the heart. Once that was done, he left Penny to close up.

Jenny was a fighter and strong.

She was doing well.

Jasmine was still in the operating room.

Penny left the postoperative unit to check on the parents.

Walter was explaining to Jenny's parents about the atrial septal defect repair. As she rounded the corner, she ran into the head of the board of directors and Walter's soon-to-be ex-wife, who was on the board. Both smiled as they ran into her.

"Ah, Dr. Burman, I was hoping to see you. How was the surgery?" Gerald asked.

"The twin Jenny is stable in the PACU right now. I'm about to check on the other twin, but Dr. Duncan is speaking with the parents. He can give you more details about Jenny's atrial septal defect." She tried to step away, because she really didn't need a run-in with Walter's ex or have it thrown in her face that she was going to withdraw her money from the hospital.

"Actually, I wanted to speak with you," Gerald said, hedging. "I feel like we've made a mistake with respect to you."

Penny's stomach knotted. "Oh?"

"We were hasty," Walter's ex, Marissa, said. "You're a remarkable surgeon, or you must be if Dr. Atticus Spike has taken a shine to you. So we want you back. We want you both here in Calgary. You and Dr. Spike."

It was everything Penny had ever wanted. Especially when she had been cast aside so roughly by the hospital that she'd considered home a little over a month ago. Except now it felt a bit hollow, and she was annoyed that they couldn't see her worth because of her own efforts. Why did it have to be tied to Atticus?

"And if Dr. Spike wants to remain in the north?"

Gerald and Marissa shared a smile. "We're going to make him an offer he can't refuse, but if he does want to stay there, then it is what it is. You've learned skills from him. We still want you back."

Penny nodded. "Before my six months arc up?"

Gerald nodded. "Of course. Now we're off to arrange a press release. Please think on it."

"I will." Penny walked away. The anxious feeling in her stomach made her a bit sick. She was glad that they wanted her back, but Atticus would never leave Fort Little Buffalo.

This is what she wanted.

The north wasn't her home.

Fort Little Buffalo wasn't where she belonged. Yet she wasn't sure Calgary was where she belonged either.

Where do you belong?

She couldn't answer that little voice, because she didn't know.

Atticus watched as the team pushed Jasmine's little gurney down the hall to the PACU. She had a long road ahead, and the next twenty-four hours were going to be dicey. All he could think about was that first treacherous twenty-four hours five years ago, when he had lost that other twin.

They had been older.

He'd had to remove dead tissue from Jasmine's intestines. There were so many other factors in the case five years ago.

Still he was worried.

It was eating away at him, and he was having a hard time shaking away those memories.

"Hey," Penny said softly.

He was relieved to see her. A familiar face in the crowd of strangers. "Hi. How is Jenny?"

"Doing well. How is Jasmine?"

"I'm on my way to speak to Georgie and Dale. The next twenty-four hours will tell. There was necrotic tissue. I had to do a bowel resection and create a stoma for now."

Penny sighed. "She's a fighter. She survived the separation and the liver resection."

Atticus nodded. "Still…"

All he could think of was the twins from five years ago. He'd thought they had been strong. Just one thing he couldn't control had gone wrong, and the same thing could happen here.

"Look, Gerald, the chief of the board of directors, wants to speak to you," Penny said, breaking through his morose thoughts. She seemed cautious, as if feeling him out.

Atticus felt his guard go up. What did Gerald want and why? Whatever it was, he didn't want it. "About what?"

"Job offers. He offered me my job back because I was working with you."

Atticus stomach knotted as he thought about what Walter had said, and he couldn't help but think of Sasha and how she'd left him once his practice in Boston had started to dwindle. It was happening again. He'd thought maybe Walter was lying, but he hadn't been.

He had let it happen again.

How could he be so foolish? He'd let his heart get involved, when he logically should've kept Penny at a distance.

He was angry.

At himself.

At her, because he'd thought she was different, but he had been a fool to let her in.

It hurt.

All of it.

"So, that's why you wanted me here?" he asked.

Penny's eyes widened. "What?"

"To further your chances of getting hired back. Walter told me the board asked you to persuade me to come here in the hopes you'd be asked back. What a coup to have me come here. You wanted me on that twin case."

"We came here because of Sophie and her biliary atresia," Penny stated. "We had no choice."

"I should've just sent you, and then some other surgeon could've handled it. I didn't need to be here. I was fool." He scrubbed his hand over his face. "You can tell Gerald I don't want the job, but I'm glad that I helped you."

"You don't sound very glad," Penny said. "And what do you mean about helping me?"

"You wanted in on the twins' case since Meridian Inlet."

"Of course I did. It's an amazing opportunity," she said hotly.

"You needed my name to be welcomed back to Calgary sooner," he snapped.

"What's wrong with you, Atticus?" she asked, her eyes filling with tears.

"I have been used before. Sasha, my ex, she just wanted me for my name."

Penny shook her head. "I'm not her."

Only he couldn't hear her, because he didn't want to.

"I don't want this!" he said. "I shouldn't have

come. I shouldn't have let you talk me into this. We shouldn't have slept together."

He could see that he was hurting her, but she had hurt him. He'd thought she was different.

He had hurt himself by getting attached to someone who he knew wasn't going to stay in the north.

Penny would stay here. She was going to leave early, and he would go back to Fort Little Buffalo, alone, and find someone to replace her.

It was better to push her away now.

"I thought you were smart?" she asked hotly. "I would never try to manipulate you. I know you didn't want to come here, but this is the opportunity of a lifetime. The press have been called. You can regain your reputation."

"The press?" he demanded. "I don't want to speak to the press! I'm not here for glory or fame. I've had that. It's not worth it. Don't you understand that prestige and fame are fleeting?"

"You did an amazing thing here today," she said. "You should take your credit."

"I did my job. I'm not here for credit or recognition. I thought you weren't either, but I was clearly wrong. You're just like the rest of them."

"How so?" she asked.

"You can't let go of your relationship with Walter. He hurt you, and yet you can't say no to him because he's top of his field."

"And you can't seem to trust anyone. You think

because one woman hurt you that we're all like that. I don't need Walter," Penny said.

"Are you sure about that?" he asked. "Why can't you see your self-worth is beyond high-profile cases and the big city?"

"Why do you believe Walter over me?" she asked sadly.

"Why didn't you tell me the truth, that you want to come back here early? You didn't have to deceive me."

"I didn't."

His face hardened, and he could tell it cut her to the quick.

"You're scared," she whispered, her voice breaking.

"I'm scared?" he asked.

"Yes."

"I'm not. I just don't need you. So I'm glad you got what you wanted from me. I'm going back home as soon as these patients are stable. Enjoy the recognition."

A tear slid down her cheek, and he regretted what he'd said in the heat of anger. He hated that he'd hurt her, but pushing her away now was for the best.

He watched Penny storm away.

She'd needed the push. He needed to sever ties.

Was it?

Fort Little Buffalo was his home, but did he

have to stay there? What was there for him, besides Horatio and his sister?

Nothing.

He was surrounded by friends and family, his work, but there was nothing for him. He was still alone in a sea of familiarity. He had no one to be his partner, but he could have Penny.

What was he so afraid of by returning to the city?

He was afraid of failing. He was afraid of Penny leaving him.

And it hit him that he had been letting fear control his life for so long. Fear had ruined his chance with the woman he was falling in love with.

The woman he was already in love with.

Penny had woken him up out of years of hiding in the dark.

And now he'd blown it.

Atticus started to follow her, but saw a nurse running from the PACU.

"Dr. Spike, it's Jasmine. Please come quick."

Atticus looked back down the hallway where Penny had disappeared. He'd make it right with her, but first, he had to save a little life.

Penny brushed away the tears that were falling. She was angry at herself for wasting tears on Atticus. What did she honestly expect? He was so scared of love, he couldn't change. Why couldn't he come to Calgary?

Why can't you go to Fort Little Buffalo?

The question caught her off guard. She had been ignoring those niggling thoughts about the north and Atticus for so long.

There was nothing holding her here.

Priyah came to visit her sometimes, but she knew she would visit her in the Northwest Territories. Her mother had moved to her grandparents' place to help after her grandfather died.

Her hands were shaking. She pulled out her phone and found a quiet place.

"Hello?"

"Hi, Mom," Penny said, her voice wobbly.

"Penny, what's wrong?" her mother asked, worried.

Penny began to cry, unable to hold it in. "Mom, I went to the north because I had an affair with a married man. I didn't know he was married, and his wife was on the board of directors. They forced me to go. Mom, I'm so sorry I let you down."

"Penny, you didn't let me down."

"No?"

"No. I'm so sorry."

"You have nothing to apologize about, Mom. You gave me the best life."

"I love you, Penny."

"I love you too, Mom." Penny sighed.

"So you've met someone up north?"

"How did you know?" she asked, confused.

"I may have made mistakes, but I know things. So what's the problem?"

"He won't take a job in Calgary."

"So? That's all?"

"Yeah."

"And you won't leave Calgary."

"Calgary has more opportunities," she said half-heartedly.

"You don't sound so sure," her mother said.

And her mother hit the nail on the head. She wasn't so sure. Fort Little Buffalo felt more like home than Calgary.

Atticus was home.

She was in love with him.

"I'm glad you told me, darling daughter," her mom said. "You know I gave up on love after your father left. I regret it. Mistakes happen. We're human, but don't harden your heart."

"Thanks, Mom."

"Come see me before you go back north. Bring this new man."

Penny smiled. "I will. If he'll have me."

Her mother snorted. "He will."

Penny sighed as she disconnected the call.

There was nothing holding her back in Calgary except memories, because this was where her parents had lived together.

This was where she had last seen her father.

He was never coming back.

And there was a man she loved who wanted to

go home to the north. Sure, the big city had more conveniences, but she was a small fish here.

There, she had more opportunities.

A part of her longed for more adventure. To go even farther and help in the remote communities. To help more people like Sophie, Jasmine, Jenny and little Marcus. Here she would have to fight for position. With Atticus, she was a teammate.

She loved him, and she was going to fight for him.

She couldn't let him go.

She was willing to risk her heart on him, and she understood why her mother had never moved on. Some people couldn't, but happily-ever-afters existed. She saw them every day. She was just so blinded by her fear.

Penny had to make things right.

She turned around and saw that Atticus was gone, but she knew where to find him. First she had to find Gerald and tell him to let Walter take over the press conference with Dr. Greene. Walter wanted that fame and recognition, so he could have it.

All Penny wanted was her own chance at happiness. All she wanted was Atticus and a home.

Atticus couldn't believe he'd said those things to Penny. Now he felt awful. His head hurt, and his stomach was twisted into knots. He hated himself for hardening his heart so much so that he'd lashed out at her.

She didn't deserve that.

His phone rang, and he glanced down to see it was Ginny calling him.

"Hello?" he answered stiffly.

"Hey, your dog bit a chunk off his kennel. He's absolutely like a wolverine or some kind of honey badger."

"He…what?" Atticus asked, confused.

Ginny laughed. "Yeah. Your dog is a real piece of work."

"Is he okay?"

"Fine. It honestly was just an excuse to call. I know you hate the city and big hospitals since Boston. I was worried about your mental health, so I wanted to check on you."

"I'm fine." He was lying, of course. He was anything but fine.

"You don't sound fine. Does this happen to be about a certain female doctor that Pamela couldn't stop gushing about?"

Atticus sighed. "I ruined things."

"Probably."

"Thanks. You're really supportive," Atticus groused.

"You know I love you, but you are a grump at the best of times. Tell me how you ruined things."

"She wants a career that the Northwest Territories can't give her." And he'd accused her of lying, but he didn't tell Ginny that.

"I see. So why don't you stay in Calgary to be with her?"

"And leave Fort Little Buffalo?"

Ginny let out an exasperated huff over the phone. "You're in love with her, so why wouldn't you?"

It hit him then. Something he never wanted to do again, because it had hurt too much when he fell for the wrong person, was give his heart to someone else. The thing was, Penny was the right person. He knew that.

Even if she wanted to stay in Calgary, he wanted her. He couldn't let her get away, and if it meant taking that job to be with her, he would.

Atticus groaned. "I think I blew my chance."

"Doubtful. Penny is not like Sasha, whom I never did like, by the way."

Atticus chuckled. "I remember."

"Fight for her, Atticus. Love with the right person is the best thing."

"Thanks, Ginny."

"For what?"

"Talking some sense into your little brother."

"Sure, just rub it in that you're younger."

Atticus chuckled. "I love you, Gin."

"Any time. We love you, Cuss. See you soon."

Atticus ended the call. He had to find Penny and make things right.

He needed Penny. He wanted a life with her.

Only her.

A PACU nurse came running towards him. "Dr. Spike!"

Atticus's stomach sank. "It's Jasmine, isn't it?"

The nurse nodded. "Her oxygen sats are low. She's not recovering well from the surgery."

As much as he wanted to find Penny and make things right, Jasmine took priority.

There was time to make things right with Penny, whereas Jasmine might not have time.

Penny got dragged into the press conference as well, but Dr. Greene and Walter did most of the talking with Gerald. After a couple hours, she was able to get away, and she made her way to the pediatric critical care unit, where she heard that Jasmine was struggling.

She walked into the room and saw the small body in the Isolette, bandaged and bruised, hooked up to wires.

And Atticus was there, watching, his head resting on his fist as he stared at the monitors. He looked up as she entered, and she was half expecting him to yell at her. Instead, his expression softened when he saw her.

"How was the press conference?" he asked.

"How did you know?"

He nodded to a television. "I watched it. You did well. Walter stole the show."

"Yes, well, he likes it. I don't, for what it's worth." She crossed her arms. "How is Jasmine?"

"Not so good." He sighed and straightened.

Her heart sank.

"What about Jenny?"

Atticus cocked an eyebrow. "What do you mean? Jenny is in the next room. She's fine."

Penny smiled as she remembered something she read. "Twins miss each other. Putting them together could help stabilize Jasmine."

His eyes widened. "Of course."

He got up and disappeared into the next room. He returned, wheeling back little Jenny. They pushed Jenny's Isolette up to Jasmine's.

"Will you help me?" he asked quietly.

"Happy to."

Together, they gently moved little Jenny and set her in the Isolette next to Jasmine. Their fingers brushed as they gingerly moved Jenny to be with Jasmine.

As they set up Jenny's monitors and fixed her cords, Jasmine's blood pressure picked up. Her heart rate stabilized. Atticus smiled.

Penny felt tears sting her eyes as she smiled, too. "Look at that."

"Good thinking." He turned to her.

"Thanks. Atticus, about…"

"No, me first. I'm sorry I said those hurtful things to you," he told her gently.

"I'm sorry for trying to push you."

"It's good you did. I was glad to be here. I wouldn't have been able to just hand off Sophie to anyone. I was meant to be here. With you. I am going to consider their offer to join Calgary."

Penny was taken aback. "What?"

"As much as I love Fort Little Buffalo, I love you more. You're my family. You're my home. So if that means I have to come here, then I will."

Penny's heart skipped a beat. "I love you too, but I don't want to stay here… The thing is, I want to go back up north."

"You do?"

"You have your nieces, and honestly, I don't know how well Horatio would do in my apartment. Your cabin is so much better."

"But your career…"

"Sure, here there's press and everything we could need, but there we can help people like Sophie and the twins. We can save lives. Together. That's what I want."

Atticus was stunned. "Truly?"

"All I want is you. I clung to Calgary in hopes my father would come back. I closed my heart to love because it never worked out, but the thing is, I think it can work with you. As long as I'm with you, I don't feel alone. I feel whole."

Atticus pulled her into his arms and kissed her.

She melted against him, knowing she was exactly where she belonged.

He was her home.

He was her heart.

EPILOGUE

Fort Little Buffalo, ten months later, July

"THAT LOOKS DUMB, Uncle Cuss."

Atticus glanced up from where he was straightening Horatio's bowtie on his collar. Horatio was sitting there so nicely, his tongue hanging out his mouth while Atticus's niece Andrea held him.

"I think it looks great," Pamela said, straightening her tiara.

Atticus winked. "Thanks, kid."

Andrea smiled slightly, but rolled her eyes in the typical way that teenagers often did. "Sure."

"He's my best man. He has to wear a bow tie." Atticus patted Horatio's head.

It was a dry, blistering hot day as they stood on the sandy shore of Pine Lake, but the heat didn't bother him one bit. They were surrounded by their friends and family for the small ceremony. People were dressed in ribbon skirts, sashes and other traditional clothing of Indigenous and Hindu culture. A mix of both worlds.

Penny had wanted to be married on a beach, and she'd picked which beach.

She wanted to be married at Pine Lake where they'd first kissed.

Thankfully, the wind kept the black flies at bay, and even though it was hot, it was still a gorgeous day.

His other niece, Sandy, began to play the wedding march on her fiddle, and his heart skipped a beat as Penny emerged from the small tent they had set up for the picnic reception afterward that was catered by Jonah.

Penny looked absolutely stunning her in her red sari, being led down the aisle by her beaming mother and grandmother.

Penny's half sister, Priyah, followed behind as maid of honor.

Penny was beaming as her mother handed her off to Atticus. He took her hennaed hands in his.

"You're trembling," Penny whispered.

"So are you," Atticus said.

"I thought surgeons were supposed to have steady hands," she teased, her eyes twinkling.

Atticus grinned. "You'll find out later how steady they can be."

Penny laughed quietly.

Horatio nosed his way in between them as the justice of the peace married them. His sister Ginny placed the blankets she had made for them around them in a Métis tradition, which united them.

"You may now kiss your bride," the justice of the peace said.

"With pleasure." Atticus pulled her close, the

blanket wrapped around them as he kissed Penny, his partner, his wife, his bride.

And he was excited to spend his life showing her just how much he loved her.

Now and forever.

* * * * *

If you enjoyed this story, check out these other great reads from Amy Ruttan

Paramedic's One-Night Baby Bombshell
A Ring for His Pregnant Midwife
Reunited with Her Surgeon Boss
Falling for His Runaway Nurse

All available now!